I N
THE
Country
Of
Salvation

IN
THE
Country
Of
Salvation

Noel Virtue

Hutchinson
London Sydney Auckland Johannesburg

This edition first published in 1990 by
Hutchinson

Century Hutchinson Ltd, Brookmount House,
20 Vauxhall Bridge Road, London, SW1V 2SA

Century Hutchinson Australia (Pty) Ltd
20 Alfred Street, Milsons Point, Sydney NSW 2061, Australia

Century Hutchinson New Zealand Limited,
PO Box 40–086, Glenfield, Auckland 10, New Zealand

Century Hutchinson South Africa (Pty) Ltd
PO Box 337, Bergvlei, 2012 South Africa

British Library Cataloguing in Publication Data

Virtue Noel, *1947–*
    In the country of salvation.
    I. Title
    823 [F]
    ISBN 0–09–174266–8

Filmset by Speedset Ltd, Ellesmere Port
Printed and bound in Great Britain by
Butler and Tanner Ltd, Frome, Somerset

To the memory of
James Keir Baxter
of Jerusalem –
Arohanui

Contents

PART ONE

Oh Shining Light 3

Bonzer Little Sunbeams 14

Up the Hill by Cable Car 24

In my Father's House 36

PART TWO

On the Land with Gumboots and Cows 49

Dying in the Night 60

In the Scorching Summer Sun 71

As Blinded Strangers 80

PART THREE

City of Sparkling Water 99

Something Unsettling in their Gaze 113

Keeping the Peace with Silence 126

With Threat of Stormy Weather 139

PART FOUR

Darkness, Coming down the Road 153

Blood of the Lamb 175

Guilt that Consumes 185

Separate Pathways 197

Ma Te Kaha Ka Ora (By Strength Survive) 211

Part One

I think it was the sea
they put inside me
when the bad blood was taken out of
my veins.
I can hear its movement
when alone.

Billy Bevan

Oh Shining Light

It bucketed down with rain most of the night. The stream opposite the house overflowed and muddy water lay across the road. At four in the morning the rain stopped. Above the range of hills on the far side of the stream cloud drifted, low, wispy and white. The rest of the sky was clear, the stars startlingly visible. Dawn was at least two hours away.

Cushla Bevan was awake and dressed by five, buttering bread and mixing fillings for sandwiches. She had put the butter on a tray near the stove. It was bitterly cold in the kitchen and the butter was hard. The house was quiet, the only sound to be heard the steady dripping of water from the gutters along the outside overhang. Away in the bush at the base of the ranges she heard a morepork calling once, then an answering cry from further away. Cushla sang softly as she worked. Words to a hymn.

There was such a lot to be done she had no idea how they would get away on time. Although the trailer was packed, the tarpaulin needed to be drawn over it and tied down. The boys' clothes needed packing. Keys to the house and the bottles of spare milk had to be taken over to Mrs Whiti next door. She was looking after Kim their cat who spent most of his time over there anyway. So that was all right.

From the bathroom there were sounds of water running and muted voices. A minute later Billy came rushing into the kitchen, still in his pyjamas.

'Oh boy, look at all the grub!' he cried. His eyes were almost popping out of his head. They gleamed. Cushla reckoned he'd had little sleep. His excitement was infectious. Their planned trip north had been hanging in the air for weeks and Billy had grizzled almost every day of those weeks, never expecting this morning to arrive.

Restel came through from the hall pulling on his oilskin. He ruffled Billy's hair.

'Don't you be impudent to your mum now,' he said, and went out the back door with a real big grin on his face. Cushla grinned too, then shared a laugh with Billy.

'I won't be imperdimp, Dad!' Billy shouted out and laughed again. Cushla went across and hugged him tightly, as he hugged her back. For some reason no one in the family could fathom, Billy would never pronounce the word properly; he misused it so often Seddon had once suggested calling him Imperdimpy Bevan.

Cushla could hear Restel in the washhouse, dragging out the trailer cover from where he'd lain it across the copper boiler. Billy had climbed up onto the bread box below the window, making a cave on the glass with his hands and peering out. He was shivering, whether from the cold or his excitement Cushla couldn't tell.

'It's stopped raining, Mum!' he shouted. 'There's water all over the blinking place but we should be all right!'

'Don't use that swear word, Billy. And stop shouting. Your dad will hear you.'

Billy turned to look at her.

'It isn't swearing, Mum,' he said. 'Seddon uses it all the time.'

She made him stand in front of the stove to put on his clothes, then he began to help her with the sandwiches, fetching, carrying, piling the dirty dishes in the sink. Cutting up pieces of greaseproof paper. The kitchen seemed warmer with him near her and now in their bedroom she could hear Seddon and Colin laughing

4

together. They would be excited too, she reckoned. It was pretty uncommon for them to have a holiday like this, money being so short and Restel having left his job. They both knew Restel would not be going back to the factory when the holiday was over. He found fault with all the places he worked in, then left, which made Cushla worried sick. They hadn't told the boys.

Billy would have his ninth birthday while they were at Lake Tutira. He was the youngest, Seddon the oldest with Colin in the middle. Each of them a real credit and she was secretly proud, despite that being a sin. Billy, inside her heart, was her special son. She told him this often, when they were alone together. Had always told him. Cushla reckoned that his redemption from having had bad blood was for some special reason. He had been born Rhesus negative, was kept in hospital for six months after his birth. The worry and fretting had given Cushla chest problems. Off and on since then she'd been chesty. Yet she loved Billy so much. Into his life as he grew up would fall blessing after blessing, and something the Lord would bestow on him, to make his light shine. He was with them now and in the future would do deeds they would all be proud of.

Billy dropped a plate onto the floor, one of a set handed down from her mum. Cushla put down the bread knife, went across to him and belted him across the head with her fist. She said nothing, and had turned back to the table when Seddon and Colin came into the room. They were punching each other on the arms and still laughing from something they'd been talking about. Billy stood staring at the back of Cushla's head.

When they finally got on the road dawn had yet to arrive. Mrs Whiti came out to her hedge to wave hooray, holding Kim in her arms. There was a faint light moving into the sky and the cloud had gone from the top of the ranges. The

Chrysler was heavily packed, the trailer behind it now covered tightly by the tarpaulin. Colin, Seddon and Billy sat high in the back seat shivering from the cold. Billy seemed to have forgotten Cushla's anger and was waving like mad to Mrs Whiti and Kim. Under his other arm he was clutching his *Coles' Funny Picture Book*. Cushla took off her scarf, patting her hair, and glanced over at Restel behind the wheel. He drove slowly from Upper Hutt, down along Waiwhetu Road, heading towards the shops and onto Wellington. From there they would cross over to the coast and up to Paraparaumu beach where they'd eat lunch. Let the boys have a swim.

As they went through Petone, passing the factory where Restel had worked, dawn appeared in a rush. The sky was still clear. The day promised to be a real scorcher.

Cushla felt pretty worn out and grateful they were on their way. Her and Restel's worries over his not having work anymore could be forgotten for a couple of weeks. They were taking enough food to last, once they'd got to the lake, and stop-offs at Radley's and then at Kitty's in Levin would tide them over for meals. The worst part of the trip would be crossing the hilly ranges after they left Levin. Cushla had packed some newspapers in case Billy was car-sick. He usually was, on the ranges. The roads, metal-chip surfaced and dusty, were narrow and never straight. She dreaded them herself.

On the Hutt Road into Wellington Restel stopped the car, pulling over onto a gravel rest place so that he could photograph the shags in the harbour. The birds were resting under the early sun with spread wings, and many were in the water, dotted about fishing. Cushla remained in the car but the boys got out with their dad. Colin and Seddon began throwing stones in the water as soon as Restel had finished. Cushla wound down the window and breathed in the ozone, grinning at Billy who was leaning over, hands on knees, staring at some wild flowers. He looked so serious, such a frown on his face it made her laugh.

6

In a minute they were all straggling back to the car, excited and refreshed by the early brightness and sharp tang of the sea air.

The beach at Paraparaumu was deserted, despite the brilliance of the midday sun. Cushla and Restel spread out blankets on the sand in front of a clump of toetoe. Each of them swam in the sea before attacking the sandwiches. Restel took a photograph of them, standing together with their togs dripping. He delayed the action and nearly knocked Cushla over rushing back from the camera, before it captured them, laughing fit to bust.

'What a blow out!' Billy said, collapsing against his mum after they'd eaten. Colin had gone down to the shore line to make a dam with the spade. Seddon was lying on his back pretending to snore while Restel moved across the beach setting up his camera, photographing herring gulls and the sun on the water.

'We have many blessings,' said Cushla. She looked over to where Restel was standing and they grinned at each other. Billy, seeing the exchange, put his arm through his mum's and squeezed.

The others out of earshot, Cushla told him, 'You're my best boy, Billy. You were spared for some purpose, something special. What do you reckon that might be?'

'Dunno,' Billy replied. Then his face lit up. 'Perhaps I'm going to be Prime Minister, eh Mum?'

Cushla grinned at him but didn't say anything.

'Boy, it's blinking hot,' Billy said, looking at his mum out of the corner of his eye. Sometimes, Billy thought, she made him feel a bit windy. She was staring at him as if she had toothache all of a sudden, or had swallowed some midges. There was a queer look on her face which made him pull away. He began to examine a shell he'd found by his foot.

*

7

Restel decided that they didn't have time to pop in and visit Cushla's brother Radley at Waikanae. He and Radley had never got on, as Cushla was all too aware. She herself reckoned there was something worrying, something not quite right about Radley but she couldn't put a finger on what it was. He'd never married and lived alone in a bach surrounded by bush. He smoked a pipe and drank beer. Whenever they had visited him in the past, Radley would stare at them all and laugh. She knew he wasn't Christian in Restel's eyes, although they'd never really discussed him. The boys thought he was the cat's pyjamas, but she, at Restel's demand, had tried to protect them from worldly influence. There was so much sin in the world it was a full-time job.

Aunt Kitty was leaning over the fence which separated her section from the one beside it when they arrived in Levin and found her new house. Each home was a good distance from the other. There were only half a dozen along the whole stretch, pretty cut off, Cushla reckoned, wondering why Kitty had picked such a spot. Kitty was talking nineteen to the dozen to a woman neighbour and didn't notice until Restel honked the horn a few times.

She burst into tears as she rushed towards them, pulling the boys to her, laughing and crying at the same time and apologizing for the mess her house was in. She had only moved down here two weeks ago, having sold her home in Palmerston North. The shifting had worn her out.

Kitty was Cushla's oldest sister, whose husband had been killed overseas while they were running a mission station in China. Cushla loved Kitty with as much desperation as she loved Billy, although Kitty had once told her she'd been bonkers to marry a bloke like Restel.

'He'll bring you nothing but tribulations, dear sister. All small men do,' she'd said. Cushla had never forgotten

the words. She didn't believe them for one minute. Restel
was a good man. Cushla knew it'd been her experiences in
China which had made Kitty change. Her and Kitty
didn't have much to do with each other anymore. Yet
because they were sisters, and loved each other, Cushla
held off from saying anything to Kitty to hurt her
whenever they did meet. After all, Kitty was dreadfully
alone, while Cushla was blessed with her boys and had
accepted Christ as her Saviour through Restel. She
rejoiced in that, believed that her path now lay alongside
his. It confused her that her brother and sister and the
adopted sister who'd run off might not be saved. For she
loved them and so prayed for their salvation, as she'd been
taught to do in church.

Aunty Kitty shooed the boys into the house. Cushla
followed, while Restel fetched the bottled quinces and
feijoas from the boot of the Chrysler. They usually
brought something for Kitty when they had a visit. She
always gave them a good feed and, as they never stayed
long, Cushla brought the offerings out of guilt as much as
love. Kitty was always so cheery, despite her past which
Cushla suspected had been chocca with sorrows.

Restel and Kitty were polite to each other but usually
there would be tension in the air which cut Cushla like a
knife. Kitty would fuss over the boys and sling off at how
big they were going to grow, like Radley, who was six foot
three and built like a ponga.

While Kitty showed Cushla and Restel over the new
house, skiting over it in her booming, musical voice, the
boys tucked into Vegemite sandwiches and two enormous
sponges filled with plum jam. There were bottles of fizzy
orangeade and a bowl full to the brim with lollies – toffees
in gaily coloured papers, gobstoppers for Billy who loved
them, and homemade raisin fudge. They were told to sit
up at the table and say grace before having a go at the
grub.

'Bless this blinking food amen,' Seddon said rapidly in

one breath when they were alone. Colin and Billy began to giggle and jostle one another.

'Boy, what a blowout!' Billy cried for the second time that day.

'We didn't stop off to see Radley,' Cushla told Kitty when they had a minute to themselves.

'You mean Restel wouldn't,' Kitty retorted. 'Hmph. Calls himself a Christian. You knew Radley was expecting you, sister. He got things in special. And he's been crook!'

To Cushla's instant look of worry Kitty said, 'Liver trouble. He may be operated on. He'll be pretty choked that you didn't stop off there. Poor bloke, his life's been one long trial.'

Cushla didn't answer. She stared out the window, wishing that Restel liked her family more.

In the end they stayed the night, after an enormous seven o'clock tea of roast lamb, fresh garden vegetables and Hokey Pokey ice-cream. Restel and Cushla had Kitty's bedroom, Kitty slept on the settee with the boys on the floor near her in their sleeping-bags. She kept them awake half the night with stories about witches and devils and silly jokes read from Billy's *Coles' Funny Picture Book*, which she referred to as his Bible. She left the back porch light on.

'In case a night creature needs me,' she told the boys mysteriously. Billy lay awake for hours longer. He felt too excited. He lay and listened to the bugs bashing into the flyscreen door, attracted by the light. He felt oddly excited by Aunt Kitty. She was so different from his mum and had such bright, sparkling eyes. And she had a wireless, which they didn't have.

'They're too worldly,' his mum had told him. 'Dad said.'

Towards dawn Billy fell asleep.

*

10

In the morning after a huge breakfast of Kornies and scrambled egg on toast and fresh cow's milk straight from the billy Aunt Kitty said a teary hooray on the front porch, as Restel wanted to get going before it was too hot.

'I reckon you'll have a bonzer time!' Aunt Kitty called as they pulled out of the drive. Restel honked the horn several times. The others waved. Billy, waving his book out the window, dropped it. Restel had to stop the car, everyone laughing. Billy fetched the book, ran back to Aunt Kitty and gave her a big smacking kiss on the lips, which made them laugh all the more.

'Hooray and bless you!' Kitty shouted.

Setting off for the longest part of the trip Restel drove east towards the Ruahine ranges, and the town of Dannevirke. Billy was car-sick and they had to stop beside the winding road while Cushla cleaned up the mess with pages from the *Evangelist*. They all had a good laugh as Billy was always car-sick and Restel cracked on that they'd used up half the newspapers in New Zealand cleaning up after him. Colin went down into a gully and picked some flowering manuka to see if it would get rid of the pong inside the car. Restel took a photograph of Billy sitting on the running board still looking crook. Then he took one of Seddon who had climbed into a macrocarpa tree pretending to be a monkey looking for nuts. Through it all they laughed fit to bust and once they were on their way again, with the windows wound down and the awful pong dispersed, they sang songs, belting out the words, and played guessing games of 'I Spy' and 'How many squashed possums can you see on the side of the road?'

In the late afternoon they had passed through Dannevirke, having stopped to eat lunch in the bush, were approaching Hastings then Napier on the Hawkes Bay coast. There they would camp for the night, before the last leg of the trip to Lake Tutira.

*

11

They arrived at the lake after nightfall, exhausted and grubby through the long haul from Napier, where they'd camped for the night at a motor lodge. Cushla had suffered two bad bouts of coughing, the fan belt on the Chrysler had broken twice and Colin as well as Billy had thrown up all over the back seat. Yet it had been a heck of a funny trip. They'd laughed such a lot, sung songs, played more guessing games inside the car along the way. By the time the tents had been erected, a large one for Cushla and Restel and a pup tent for the boys, it was well after midnight. Across the lake drifted strange noises, grunting of wild pigs and cries of moreporks. It disturbed none of them from their sleep, except for Billy. The night was crisp, the stars above them so bright with the moonlight to enhance it.

As he was acting cranky because of the cramped space in the pup tent, Cushla let Billy sleep in the car with the windows open. The pong was still there but he didn't mind. He woke shivering, more from excitement than the cold, after a few hours. The tents were dark, he could hear someone snoring as he crept out of the car and walked down to the edge of the water, peering at the wisps of mist which lay across it reaching upward to touch the night sky. Around him he could hear the bush rustling and twigs snapping and low snuffling noises.

Billy was still awake at dawn, staring out across the water, sitting on an old log with a blanket round him, when Cushla got up to boil water for tea on the paraffin burner. She stood watching him quietly. His small, tousle-haired figure caused her heart to pound with love.

Then Cushla stumbled, reached out to grip the side of the tent, for there appeared then to overwhelm her some dark future vision which made her body tremble and legs weaken. She wrenched her sight away from Billy, forced her eyes to stare elsewhere.

12

Billy turning his head, seeing her there so distraught, let the blanket drop from his shoulders. He ran to her side, hugging her tightly, pressing himself against her. Cushla stood unable to return the embrace, her head turned away.

They were there, Billy peering up at his mum's averted face, when Seddon and Colin emerged from their tent in swimming togs. Leaping, whooping and shouting with joy they raced past the two motionless figures, threw themselves into the water as the sun began to rise up into the sky from the far edge of the lake, to cast its shining light.

Bonzer Little Sunbeams

'It's a game,' Seddon told Billy. 'Put your arms round my neck.' Seddon had come out of the bathroom, still wet from a bath. He had a towel wrapped round his waist and his penis was sticking out, pushing the towel away from him. Billy giggled when he saw it. He'd been sitting on the settee looking at his *Coles' Funny Picture Book* when Seddon came into the living-room. Colin was in bed crook with a bad cold. Mum and Dad were up at the church. Outside the house a storm was brewing. Across the sky forked lightning split the fast moving cloud. A month had gone by since the holiday at Lake Tutira.

Billy wore his new pyjamas, which had once been Seddon's, then Colin's. They were patched and cut down to Billy's size. He slid off the settee and came over to where Seddon was standing.

'Go on,' Seddon said. 'I won't hurt you.'

Billy thought Seddon was breathing a bit funny as if he'd just run a race. As Billy put his arms round Seddon's neck then wrapped his legs round Seddon's waist the towel came loose and fell to the floor.

'Slide down me,' said Seddon in a cracked voice. 'Slide down to the floor then do it again.'

Billy was sitting on the floor at Seddon's feet when Colin wandered in, his eyes half-closed from sleep. He stood staring with his mouth open. Seddon had half-turned towards him as he'd entered and Colin's eyes were on Seddon's penis which was bright pink like his face. Billy was sliding his hand up and down it, quite unaware that Colin had come in.

'I'm telling on you!' Colin said in a loud voice. 'I'm going to tell Mum!'

Seddon's face went scarlet. He grabbed the towel from the floor and ran back to the bathroom, slamming the door and locking it. They were each supposed to lock the door whenever they had a bath. Billy tried to stand up then almost fell, feet caught in his pyjama trousers which had come loose. He began to giggle.

'You'd better get to bed, Billy,' Colin told him. 'Mum and Dad will do their blocks if you're still up when they get back.'

Billy picked up his book from where it lay on the settee and went off towards his room. Seddon was still in the bathroom. Billy tried to open the door but it was locked. He felt peculiar, a little bit scared. There were butterflies in his tummy. He had no real understanding of what had just happened but he'd felt important. He wouldn't have minded it happening again.

'I enjoyed that game!' he shouted through the bathroom door keyhole. 'Can we have another go?'

There was no reply.

Seddon and Colin shared a bedroom. Billy had a smaller one to himself at the back of the house. It had always been that way, Billy sleeping on his own because Cushla claimed he was special. It was a railway house, which Restel rented in Upper Hutt not far from the church. They had lived in so many houses all over Wellington and the Hutt valley Billy couldn't remember half of them. He'd been born at Day's Bay in the big hospital near the beach, had remained in hospital for six months, having had all his blood changed, so he was special. His photograph had been in the newspaper. His mum told him that on the day she was allowed to take him home she took him across the road onto the beach so he could breathe in the ozone. Billy loved the sea from then on.

'Remember, Billy,' Cushla would tell him many times over, 'I reckon the Lord has saved you for something special.'

'Am I more special than Seddon and Colin?' Billy sometimes asked.

'I love all you boys,' Cushla would reply, grinning, giving him a hug, 'but you're my little sunbeam.'

Restel had brought home a wireless. He would have been too windy to buy one if Cushla hadn't nagged for it – for the boys, of course, not really for her. It was similar to the one they'd looked at in the window of a shop at Dannevirke, where they'd stopped on the way home from Lake Tutira. Already Aunt Bulla had complained about it. She was Restel's older sister who lived in a flat at Epuni. She went to church in Wellington and was more narrow-minded than her brother.

'It's sinful,' she'd said to Restel about the wireless. 'Not only that, it's a danger to the boys. I read that the air-waves can float out and damage your brain. I am ashamed for you, Restel. I can't let it be switched on when I visit. Goodness knows what the Lord Jesus Christ thinks of you.'

Aunt Bulla was a spinster, had never thought of marriage, wore her hair in a bun at all times, didn't wear make-up nor nylon stockings (she wore socks) and was forever talking of the Old Country, where people had known how to worship the Saviour.

'They are heathens here,' she would tell Cushla. 'Sinners with wicked ways. You must protect the boys. They are God's little sunbeams!'

The wireless was very tall and sat in the corner of the living-room beside the settee. It had four dials and an oval

16

plastic station-finder which glowed when it was switched on. The boys were real keen on it, especially Seddon. He would often crouch in front of the wireless for hours at night, before bedtime. He liked the news most of all, especially the world news, spoken from England in a strange plummy accent. He made Billy laugh by squeezing his nostrils and saying, 'This is the BBC World Service.'

Whenever Aunt Bulla came Cushla would cover the wireless with a sheet, and Seddon began to spend the time she was there in his bedroom, sulking.

'You can listen to it on other nights,' Restel told Seddon. 'Bulla's my sister and I have to respect her.'

Yet the wireless became a focus for each of them, drawing them together. Most nights they would all sit round it, Restel in his favourite chair beside the fire, Colin and Seddon on the floor, Billy curled up on the settee with Cushla who sat darning socks. Seddon would sit picking fluff from the insides of his slippers. Colin would often bring in his Meccano set and build things. He was clever with his hands. The Meccano set had been Restel's, given to him when he was a boy, and brought out from the Old Country when his parents shifted to New Zealand. Slowly they'd added pieces to it, and now it was kept in a wooden box Colin had made at school. Billy never touched the Meccano. He wasn't allowed. Privately he thought it was stupid anyway. He enjoyed looking at books far more, even *Popular Mechanics* magazines which Restel brought home from the office. Restel was a clerk now, in a Jantzen factory. There was, however, less money and the expense of getting the wireless had scared Restel stiff. Yet the nights when they sat round it made him thankful that the bloke at work, who'd sold it to him on the cheap, had done him a greater favour than he'd realized.

Restel was hoping that Seddon would get saved soon. He was already showing signs of manhood and was leaving school within the month. That on the one hand he welcomed, but also feared.

17

'It's living here,' Restel began to say to Cushla. 'The city. It's all right for Bulla and us but the boys are heading off to a difficult age. We need to be closer to the Lord, in the country somewhere. There'll be less sin there.'

Cushla felt she had to agree, but didn't have any notion how they could go about it. They had no money saved and Restel had spent his bonus on the wireless.

'Perhaps I could find a job,' she suggested.

Restel frowned and shook his head. 'I'm not having you working,' he told her. 'Your place is here at home. I'm the bread winner. We'll manage.'

Cushla knew he'd had an idea for weeks but wouldn't discuss it with her. She kept quiet, after asking him once. He'd told her that he was communing with the Lord, who would give him an answer.

'You must pray too, Cushla,' he said. 'That's what I want you to do. Pray for guidance and make certain the boys don't stray off the road. Seddon needs watching. I saw him leering at a girl the other Sunday, at church. We can't have anything filthy going on.'

He would never be specific about rude things, Cushla had learned. Even when they had relations he'd insisted on the light being off, and most of their clothes on. They had never seen each other's naked bodies. He had slapped her once, when she'd made approaches. Had told her that such forwardness was wrong from women, that such acts were for men to decide over, when another child was needed.

'Anything else is the sin of lust, Cushla. You will have to fight your desires, and pray they'll be taken from you.'

He rarely hugged her in front of the boys, rarely kissed her when they were alone. Lately she'd begun to have such dreams. She would wake up hot and irritable and find herself snapping at Billy or Colin, who were often up to tricks and needed a good telling off. She would get in such a paddy over their behaviour, it would frighten her. If she'd thought about it, she would have blamed Restel.

18

Instead she prayed and sang hymns, when alone in the house and feeling the strain of her longings. Praying and singing hymns was the way to a peaceful heart, she'd been told. But she still couldn't help feeling lonely.

Cushla enjoyed going to church on Sundays although the evening service was often full of hoity-toity women she didn't like. A lot of them didn't go to the morning service and she'd always wondered why. Her, Restel and the boys went at least twice on Sundays. Each of the boys attended Bible class and Sunday school. She was real proud when Seddon came home and recited all the books of the Bible to her. She had given him a shilling. Billy's Sunday school drawings she had pinned up above the door of the safe, in the kitchen. One was especially good, of Jesus surrounded by little kiddies. Aunt Bulla had been real shook over that.

'You shouldn't let him draw our Lord,' she said when she saw it. 'Whatever will he be doing next? That's sinful, Cushla. It's taking the Lord's image in vain. You mustn't allow it. We'll have to keep an eye on you, sister!'

She turned to Restel. 'It's New Zealand I blame. The Maoris too, of course. They've influenced us far too much. Lackadaisical lot, if you ask me. You mark my words, brother, there is sin and sloth everywhere in this country.'

Cushla didn't point out that Billy had done the drawings at Sunday school.

Despite his deep love for Bulla, Restel was scared of her. So to help make it up to her he decided they would go on a picnic to Petone beach. He'd been fretting that Bulla might get even more shirty over the wireless.

They planned the picnic for a Saturday. Cushla worried herself sick for days over how she was expected to manage. Restel made certain she had enough for food normally but a picnic was a picnic. As it worked out, Billy let it slip when Bulla brought round the yellow-jacketed *Daily Mirror*s which came from England. The picnic was meant to be a surprise for her. Bulla immediately took charge when she heard and the following morning brought round so much food and extra bread Cushla felt swamped, and somewhat humiliated, though she didn't show it.

Billy helped her in the kitchen making up sandwiches and filling the three thermos flasks with tea. Colin and Seddon helped their dad pack the car, and because it was a scorcher they all put their togs on underneath their clothes, so they could have a swim as soon as they arrived. Restel packed a folding chair for Bulla to sit on, and Cushla took along her brolly, as Bulla hated sitting in the sun for long.

She was waiting outside when they drove up to her flat, wearing her woollen coat buttoned up to the neck and her black straw hat with the pins which Seddon always reckoned looked like swords. She hadn't brought anything with her apart from a towel to wipe her feet, and a handbag over her arm.

'I love a paddle,' she told them, sitting erect in the high back seat of the Chrysler. She disapproved of swimming.

'They pump all sorts of nasty stuff into the water,' she added. 'I'm not at all surprised that people get crook, and with this heat,' and she began to fan her face with a hanky. She grinned at Seddon and Colin sitting beside her. Billy was in the front.

'I've brought some lollies for you boys,' she told them. 'Special ones from the shops. Pineapple chunks and chocolate fish. You can eat them after lunch.' She began to laugh. 'Only fish you'll see today. All the gunge in the water knocks them off.'

For the journey, despite it being short, she produced a huge bag of mixed gobstoppers, aniseed balls and jaffas, and they all tucked in, Billy making them laugh as he stuffed two gobstoppers in at once then kept taking them out of his mouth to see the colours change, producing dreadful slobbering noises. By the time they arrived at the

20

beach their spirits were high. Aunt Bulla said she really needed a lie down, she'd had such a good laugh.

Restel and Colin spread out the trailer tarpaulin on the sand in front of a paling fence, as a wind had sprung up. They hauled everything from the car, laughing all the time, making Aunt Bulla comfortable, Cushla's brolly within reach in case she got too hot. Bulla sat stiffly in the chair, her coat still buttoned. She stared out at the water.

'Our Lord Jesus Christ has touched this country,' she said. 'In all the world he has put his touch on New Zealand and made it his own.'

They were used to her contradictions and Cushla even found them funny, when Bulla was being cheerful. She could make them all scared stiff with one glance when she was being cranky but her generosity was boundless. Her faith was strong, and never wavered. Cushla had often wondered if she was lonely, living the way she did. Yet it didn't show, and her aloneness had not made her hoity-toity. She could be a dragon, but was always straight-forward. She worshipped the boys.

Bulla sat watching them having a swim in the sea, surrounded by midges which she attempted to belt with the brolly. She waved to the boys and applauded their feats in the water, Billy doing handstands in the shallows, Seddon pretending to be a porpoise and Colin attempting to lift his dad up onto his shoulders, with hilarious results and much splashing. Cushla remained submerged up to her neck as she felt a bit put out by Bulla's frank stares. Bulla didn't approve of women showing their bare skin in public.

Along the beach other families were gathered. Small kiddies were running about in the nuddy with tin buckets and spades. Far out on the water were dotted a multitude of yachts and other sailing craft. Despite the wind the sun was boiling. Cushla watched as Bulla stood up and took off her coat. She began to set out the sandwiches, cakes and cold cooked sausages on tin plates across the tarpaulin, ready for lunch. Across the calm water came Bulla's voice singing a hymn. Behind her, high up in the clear pale blue, a hawk was hovering. For the first time in weeks Cushla felt almost content, blessed by a family she loved.

Three days after the picnic Restel caught Billy in the bathroom rubbing himself up and down the rim of the bath, over which he'd placed a towel. He had been in there so long without the sound of water running Restel opened the door quietly and peered in, annoyed that the door wasn't locked as he insisted.

At first glance he couldn't figure out what Billy was doing, until Billy sat up and examined his penis with great concentration, then, a little frown coming over his face, he recommenced his game, lying on his tummy, quite naked, rubbing himself urgently along the bath towel. When he looked up and saw his Dad watching he froze, going beetroot in the face. Restel moved into the room and closed the door behind him, locking it.

Cushla couldn't believe the screams when she first heard them. She'd been out back filling up the concrete tub with buckets of water and dropped the bucket, it gave her such a shock. Water splashed all over her legs. She ran across the grass patch to the back door and pounded on the bathroom door with her fists when she found it locked. Restel immediately opened it and moved past her, stony-faced and pale. He appeared to be holding up his strides with both hands.

She found Billy lying up against the wall, still crying out in a hideous fear. Across his bottom and legs were ugly red marks and beside him lay Restel's leather braces. Cushla gathered Billy into her arms, carrying him to his room and laying him on the bed. She was horrified at the marks on his body.

Later she suffered the worst bout of chesty coughing she'd ever suffered since the shock of hearing about Billy's bad blood.

It was the severest belting Restel had given any of the boys. Cushla did not know why he'd belted Billy so violently and Restel wouldn't tell her, refused to discuss the matter, which added to her stress. Cushla attempted to ask Billy what had happened but he was so shook he could barely speak to any of them. Seddon spent a lot of time with him, in Billy's room. She listened to their murmuring voices on the other side of the door with a kind of resentment building inside her which made her want to shake Billy whenever she saw him, during the following days. Something, a feeling she couldn't understand, stopped her from asking Seddon. The desire to shake Billy scared her, as it was so strong. Her breathing remained laboured because of that. She went about the house with a heavy step.

In the evenings, while they sat listening to *Life with the Lyons* or some other heck of a funny programme she could never remember the name of, Billy would sit on the floor very close to Seddon, almost touching, staring up into his face with a quiet trust.

Up the Hill by Cable Car

Colin had been playing footy with some boys from school, pretending they were an All Blacks team, when his wrist was cracked. He was a real sporty type, tall and broad shouldered. With his ginger hair and wide lips, Cushla reckoned he would grow up pretty handsome. He told Cushla that one of the boys had stomped on his wrist, calling him a 'blinking holy roller'. Restel had rushed Colin off to the hospital, and they'd kept him there overnight, which he'd thought a bit of a dag. The wrist was encased in plaster when he came home and Billy had been the first to sign it. Billy felt pretty proud of that as he knew Colin reckoned he was a bit of a sissy. Colin was a monitor at school and wouldn't have anything to do with Billy when they were there. Billy hated sport and never played any games if he could get out of them. Colin played games all the time. Once when Billy was being bullied by some bigger boys he went to Colin who was on duty in the playground and had a moan. Colin told him to bugger off and not to be such a sissy.

'I'm telling on you for swearing,' Billy had said, feeling hurt. Colin had turned his back.

Outside school Colin wasn't at all fascinated by Billy as Seddon had begun to be. Nothing was ever said about the game Colin had witnessed, but it caused changes.

Already having been told he was special by Cushla, Billy relished the attention Seddon gave him. Cushla hardly noticed, believing that the boys had always got on. She had other worries. Restel's job with Jantzens proved to be a bit risky as they were laying people off and the money he was paid went nowhere. Cushla spent hours now darning socks and mending clothes after washing them by hand instead of in the copper boiler, to save the electric. With Colin home from school for a while until his plastered wrist was a bit better, then Billy going down with a cold which she supposed he'd caught from Colin who was still sniffing, her chest seemed even worse. Confined to the house she reckoned she was going crackers.

A week later, in the middle of the BBC World News, the wireless blew up. It was the biggest fright any of them had ever had. Aunt Bulla, when she heard about it, reckoned that the Great Redeemer had not meant them to have the wireless, and the fright they'd all been given when it exploded was His judgement on the matter.

Cushla missed the wireless. It had helped her relax. They all missed it, although that was never discussed. What had been left of it Restel had carted off in the Chrysler to the dump, and the wooden casing he'd chopped up for firewood. It'd been too far gone to be repaired.

'Waste not, want not,' he said grinning as he piled up the chopped wood in the washhouse.

'It won't burn,' Cushla told him. 'Varnished wood won't burn.'

'Nonsense,' he said. 'We can't afford to waste any-thing.'

Cushla had begun to save up some of her housekeeping money, and privately planned a trip into Wellington, with Colin and Billy, on the train. She wanted to tell Billy who was real brassed off getting over his cold but daren't as he'd get too excited and blab it to Seddon in front of their dad. Billy seemed to confide everything to Seddon these days. Restel had told her that it wasn't healthy they spent so much time alone together.

'Seddon needs some mates his own age,' he'd begun to

say. 'There's some good young people up at the church.'

Seddon had come out for Jesus Christ at a recent service and Restel was so pleased he'd bought him a bike. Seddon had left school now, had begun working his apprenticeship as a mechanic at a garage in Naenae, and needed a bike to get there. Where the money had come from for the bike Restel wouldn't tell Cushla. She suspected it had been from Bulla. Cushla planned to take Colin and Billy into the city so they wouldn't feel left out.

'If I get saved can I have a bike?' Billy had asked her. Cushla had belted him across the legs, she'd been so shocked at that. She didn't explain anything as Billy was too young to understand. They have to learn, she thought afterwards, feeling guilty about hitting him in a paddy.

Restel gave Seddon bike lessons up and down the road outside the house, on Saturday afternoons when he came home from the factory. Billy watched, hiding behind the hedge. Seddon hadn't wanted anyone watching. Billy had a good hiding place. With his friend Jeffrey he sometimes hid behind the hedge to wait for the nuns to go past. Further along the road was a convent. When the nuns came down the road Billy and Jeffrey, crouching as low as they could, would shout out at the tops of their voices, 'Penguins!' and then run away giggling, usually down the side of the house and round the back to the washhouse to hide. After the first few times the nuns guessed they were there and would call out, 'We can see you little boys!' in cheery voices even before they had reached the hedge. Billy thought the nuns must be a bit of all right but he'd been taught that Catholics were bad and nuns were wicked women. It confused him.

Jeffrey was Billy's best friend. He talked in a real flash accent and had only been in New Zealand a year, having come out from a place called Plymouth in the Old Country. Jeffrey wasn't supposed to visit Billy's house but he did, on his bike. Sometimes they went to Jeffrey's house

26

when his mum was out, to listen to their radiogram which also played records.

Billy had told Jeffrey about his game with Seddon, which had happened a few times now, and they'd giggled a lot over what it meant. Sometimes they would rub each other through their shorts but nothing ever happened and they got bored and sore.

'We'll have to wait till we're bigger,' Billy said.

A little while after that Billy was given a hiding and told he wasn't allowed to mix with Jeffrey, as his parents were not saved and didn't even go to any church.

In the evenings Cushla, Restel and the boys began to play board games, now the wireless had gone. There was no chance of their getting another one. They also looked forward to Aunt Bulla's visits. She came over pretty often now and nearly always brought lollies for the boys and *Daily Mirror*s in the yellow paper jackets and food. Billy would lie on the floor reading the comic strips and looking at the pictures of the Old Country. Aunt Bulla would sit herself down in the middle of the settee, her huge handbag on her lap, and talk away nineteen to the dozen.

'I'm real proud that Seddon has got saved,' she would say. 'All his sins have been washed away in the blood of the lamb. This is God's own country. I asked Mr Bremner at my church to pray for all of you. He's a fine Christian man, Mr Bremner, even if his son has gone to the dogs.'

'Seddon got a bike for getting saved, Aunty,' Billy said, looking up from his reading. 'I hope I get one too, a real beauty one, when I'm saved.'

'Don't be impudent, Billy!' Restel said. 'Seddon needs his bike for his job.' He and Bulla swapped a look, which told Cushla where the money had come from.

'How are your bowels, Cushla?' Bulla asked in a loud voice.

Cushla didn't reply.

'Billy's not imperdimp, Dad!' Seddon said with a huge grin on his face. Everyone had a laugh at that. Aunt Bulla handed round her bag of lollies for the umpteenth time. She'd brought a banana cake too and some savaloys, which Cushla said later ponged as if they'd been kept in her wardrobe. They ponged to high heaven of moth balls. The cake was all right, though. They all tucked into it once Bulla had gone home. Billy reckoned Aunt Bulla made the best banana cake in the whole of New Zealand.

'Boy, am I stuffed,' Seddon said after and Restel had a go at him for swearing.

They were not allowed playing cards, which were sinful and worldly and used for gambling, so the games they played were Snakes and Ladders and Ludo, which were kept in an old cake tin. Some nights there were prayer meetings held at the house when all the church people came and piled into the living-room. Because Restel and Cushla were usually too short, couldn't afford any extra food, the visitors brought their own. The boys were confined to their rooms on the prayer meeting nights but would sneak out to the kitchen and pinch the sandwiches, taking them back to Billy's room where they'd sit on the bed and have a blow-out with the lights off. Billy was supposed to be asleep by then. No one said anything and there was even food left over which Cushla would put in their lunch tins for school the next day. Seddon began to call those nights 'the miracle of the loaves and fishes' but not in front of his dad. He would make Billy laugh by pretending to make the sandwiches double in number.

'Jesus did that when He was here,' he'd say.

'Did He live in Upper Hutt?' Billy asked. Colin and Seddon laughed fit to bust over that so loudly, then began to have a pillow fight and Restel had come in to see what was going on. He'd stared at the sandwiches spread all over Billy's bed, then went out without saying a word.

Cushla told Seddon the next morning that he'd been real wild at them but she'd stopped him from giving them hidings. She was scared stiff of that now, since Billy's bad belting. She'd still not found out why it had happened.

'I told him, Seddon, I told him. It's not your fault we're too short to buy flash food like that. You're good boys, it isn't stealing.'

Restel had been offered extra work at the factory on Sundays, but wouldn't work then because he was a Christian. Cushla tried to talk him into it.

'We can't go on like this, Restel,' she said. 'The boys need new clothes, their shoes are all worn out. And what if they get real crook, eh? What then? Tell me that one. We're living on the bread line. Men do work on Sundays. The Lord wouldn't get all het up about it, I'm sure of it. We're the only ones in the road who are always short. People look at me in queer ways. Mr Johnson at the grocer's won't give me any more credit.'

Restel had been real shook over that. He'd had no idea that Cushla couldn't make ends meet.

'You're shaming me, Cushla. You're not to ask for credit again, do you hear me? It's wicked and sinful. I'll speak to Bulla if you can't manage. I don't know what you do with the money I give you.'

'I don't want Bulla knowing,' Cushla said. 'She brings over enough stuff as it is.' Cushla wanted to say something about Seddon's bike, but bit her tongue and kept quiet.

'I'm not having you run up bills!' Restel told her. 'Bulla wants to help, she has a bit tucked away. As a Christian I won't work on the Lord's day. There's an end to it.'

Cushla still didn't let on about the trip to Wellington she was planning. She had enough now for their fares and extras. They could take some sandwiches and there were a

few shillings each for Colin and Billy to have a shout – buy
something from the shops like new Meccano pieces or a
couple of books. She began to get pretty excited about it.
Restel kept asking why she was in such a good mood.

'You have to be cheery,' she told him. 'We have to
count our blessings. He watches over us. If I wasn't
cheery I'd lose my marbles.'

When the big day came Cushla got up and pretended
everything was normal, getting breakfast as usual dressed
in her nightie and an overcoat and thick socks because the
air was so chilly. Restel left for work earlier on certain
days, to catch the bus instead of using the Chrysler, long
before the boys were up and while it was still dark. She
went to kiss him on the lips when he left but he drew back
and frowned at her. She watched him walking up the path
to the road with a mixture of nervy heart and excitement
inside her, the expectancy of telling Colin and Billy where
she was taking them causing her heart to flutter. Cushla
knew Seddon wouldn't fret. He hated the shops, thought
going out with his mum now was sissy. Besides that, he
worked every day and couldn't stay home as he often had
when he was at school. He was getting to be a beaut little
man, going off each morning in his overalls.

She waited until they were sitting at the table eating
Kornies before telling them. Billy became so excited he
knocked over his glass of milk yet Cushla was blowed if
she could get wild over that. Seddon helped her clean up
the mess while Billy went to change into his clothes. Milk
had splashed all over the floor as well as over his pyjamas
and over Cushla. Colin didn't say much, just sat there
beaming. He would occasionally stutter quite badly when
he got excited and it shamed him. He'd learned to keep
quiet but his grin said everything.

Cushla allowed Seddon to go off to his new job on his
bike, probably against Restel's wishes as he hadn't
learned to use the bike properly yet, but it was a special
day and she wanted each of the boys to be happy. It was

real bedlam for the half-hour before they left. Billy racing round the house hurrying them all up and giving shouted reports on the weather. Seddon unable to find his bike pump and turning out all the drawers in his tallboy looking for it, and Colin deciding that he would make up the sandwiches. Getting Vegemite everywhere and sheets of crumpled greaseproof paper all across the kitchen floor. Forgetting the butter by the stove which melted and ran across the warped lino. By the time they were all dressed up and raring to go Cushla felt worn out but so happy at the boys' excitement she held them to her at the door, hugging them as they hugged her. They walked up the path with Seddon careering in and out between them on his bike, all of them laughing like mad and Billy chattering non-stop, hardly pausing for breath.

Once they'd waved hooray to Seddon they walked down to the school where Cushla left notes in the letter-box explaining that her two boys were crook. Then they caught the bus down to Lower Hutt. Cushla had watched Seddon biking off up the street anxiously but he seemed to have mastered the bike. Colin reckoned he looked pretty grown up in his khaki overalls and cap, pedalling away so hard it was enough to bust his boiler.

The day was overcast with a typical southern wind, but little risk that it would bucket down with rain as the wind would keep it away. After the bus ride the modern electric train they caught from Lower Hutt sped them alongside the harbour road and Colin and Billy spent the trip deciding what they could buy with the money their mum had given them. Cushla sat having a good yarn with a woman she used to know at Day's Bay who'd moved to Johnsonville and had come down to visit her sister who'd got TB.

Billy couldn't decide what he wanted to buy. He wouldn't have minded a *Radio Fun* annual but that clashed with getting a *Famous Five* book. He reckoned the *Famous Five* were beaudy, especially the girl called George, who he thought was a bit of a dag. Of course, he could buy lots of lollies but they wouldn't last. Colin decided straight away that he had enough for a clockwork motor which was in the Mecanno catalogue Restel had brought home.

'My eldest boy's started work now, Penelope,' Cushla was telling her friend. 'He's become a real little man. I'm so proud of him!'

They walked from Wellington railway station, down Lambton Quay, looking in all the shop windows. Billy reckoned he'd never seen so many people.

'The whole blinking world must be here, Mum!' he said in a loud voice and some bloke stopped and patted him on the head and gave him sixpence. Grown-ups tended to do that a lot, Billy had noticed. They never did it to Colin. Cushla went bright scarlet in the face. She made Colin and Billy hold onto her, which Colin was a bit put out by.

'I'm no sissy, Mum,' he grizzled.

They soon cheered up when she said they were heading for the cable car, would have a go on it all the way to the Observatory on top of the hill, where they could admire the view.

'What's an obs . . . observa. . . ?' Billy asked, struggling over the word.

'It's like a lavatory,' said Colin and he and Billy went off in a fit of giggles. When they'd calmed down Cushla explained, just as they arrived at the shopping arcade from where the cable car left. The boys had never been on it and looked at the steep rails with their eyes boggling and their mouths open.

'You'll catch flies, you two will,' said the man who sold the tickets. Cushla got them on board and let them sit on an outside seat so long as they held on tight and didn't wriggle about. She worried about Colin's wrist in the cast but a trip out was a trip out, and the day mustn't be spoiled. Privately Cushla was terrified of the cable car and went most of the way up to the top with her eyes shut. It was lucky there were only a few people aboard. At each stop she'd open her eyes and pretend she was having as good a time as the boys, ducking her head and grinning when they looked in to see if she was all right. They craned their necks so much Cushla was scared stiff they'd rick them. Billy couldn't stop peering back to where they'd come from, rapidly becoming so far below them and so steep he kept asking Colin why the cable car didn't slide back.

When they alighted at the top the sun was peeking out between cloud and despite the fierce wind they stood on the grassy hill, looking down across the harbour and to the right where the tall wooden houses rested on the slopes. A sight which never failed to grip Cushla by the heart, it was all so beaut. How she loved the Wellington hills.

The boys wanted to explore but as she'd planned the whole day and wanted the surprises to go without a hitch they went down on the cable car again, after a short wander and a look at the Observatory. The boys sat inside the car with her going down so she had to keep her eyes open. Clutching her handbag and the tin of sandwiches tied with string, her gaze remained firmly fixed on the seats in front. She kept a brave grin on her face, and sighed with relief when the car got to the bottom. Feeling a little dizzy when they clambered off, Cushla reckoned they could eat their lunch early, sitting watching the cars leaving and arriving. The comings and goings seemed to overwhelm Colin with fascination. He wanted to make a cable car out of his Meccano when they got home, once he'd bought the clockwork motor.

'Boy,' he kept saying, 'it's sure a clever thing.'

After they'd finished the sandwiches Cushla went over to a shop and brought back three milkshakes and several straws. She asked the lady to do different flavours and they each had a taste before deciding which one they liked best. Colin and Billy made her laugh like anything as they kept blowing through the straws and causing froth to bubble up, but she hurried them now, folding the greaseproof papers back into the tin so she could use them again for school lunches.

'Where're we going now, Mum?' asked Billy. 'Can we get to the shops now? I'm going to buy a *Famous Five* book and Colin wants a motor.'

They wandered down to Willis Street and while the boys looked in the window of a model shop, Cushla, keeping a close eye on them, checked the performance times at the Majestic Picture House, then went smartly back so Colin could go in and buy his clockwork motor. Then off to buy Billy's *Famous Five* book (he couldn't decide which one he wanted and Cushla flew into a bit of a panic over the time), got back outside the Majestic a few minutes before two, when the picture show was to begin.

Her guilt over taking them to the pictures was squashed by the boys' reaction when she led them up the steps and into the foyer. Billy at first looked a bit cranky as he thought the building was some kind of huge church. Then, when he knew, he started to chatter away and hardly stopped until she paid for the tickets and took them through the swinging doors into the auditorium with its posh drapes and coloured lights and dozens of happy people. Both the boys were struck dumb.

Goodness knows what Restel will say, she thought. She knew she would have to tell him, she couldn't lie. She sat through the shorts and then the interval feeling quite windy (there wasn't enough money for ice creams yet the boys didn't notice) but by the time the main picture began she sat back in the comfy seat and relaxed, became so taken in by it all she felt herself transported, her heart uplifted in love when she watched the boys' faces out of the corner of her sight.

The big film was called *The Court Jester*, with Danny

Kaye and Basil Rathbone. It was quite all right for the boys to watch. Parts of it were so exciting Billy jumped up and down in his seat and an usherette with a torch came and asked Cushla in a loud whisper, a grin on her face, to keep the little bloke quiet a bit.

'I'm sorry, I'm so sorry,' Cushla kept whispering, even after the usherette had gone, so intent was her gaze on the screen. What a handsome brute that Basil Rathbone was. And didn't Danny Kaye have such gorgeous hair.

It was all over far too soon and when they came out into the street Cushla saw it was nearly five o'clock and Restel would be home before them. They were halfway down to the railway station when Billy realized he didn't have his book with him. He reckoned he'd left it on the seat next to where he'd sat. He began to bawl his eyes out. Cushla dragged them back to the picture house and found the nice usherette who was so concerned she took Billy in with her and he not only found his book but saw part of the newsreel again. He came out beaming and rushed to Cushla and Colin without thanking the kind lady. By the time Cushla made him thank her, and they'd started off again, reached the station, waited for a train, got on a bus at Lower Hutt and walked home at the other end, it was dark. Cushla was pretty shook up and felt her chest getting tight as they entered the house. She was shaking with nerves at what Restel was bound to say.

He was sitting at the table eating bread and dripping and drinking tea.

'Where on earth have you been?' he said loudly to her, glaring. There was no sign of Seddon.

'We've been to the pictures, Dad!' Billy shouted. 'It was real beaut. Can we go again next week?'

Restel stood up. His face had gone a deep red. He started to shout and didn't stop for minutes. Cushla hung her head. She said nothing.

In my Father's House

The church was packed out, not a seat to spare. Most of the younger kiddies had been shunted down to the front to sit on the floor and along the sides, although Cushla had kept Billy and Colin with her. Restel was on the far side with the men, as he was going to give a talk. Seddon had sat with the bigger boys at the back. They were all spruced up, faces shining, wearing their best clobber. Seddon was wearing his first pair of strides, grey serge, and Restel had loaned him a tie. They had sung several hymns already and Billy was getting fidgety, picking at a scab on his knee and trying hard not to giggle at the faces Colin was pulling when their dad wasn't looking over.

Restel was still a bit het up about their having gone to the pictures, although that was ages ago now. He hadn't said much to Cushla about it, after he'd shouted, but he had told her that to make up for her backsliding she should bear witness for Jesus tonight, at the special service, when people were asked to. That would be near the close when they'd sing 'Just as I am, without one plea' which always got people going so she wouldn't be alone standing down the front. She knew she had sinned against Restel as well as against the Lord, but surely to have given the boys such a good day had not been all wrong. Colin and Billy still talked about the trip out, wanted to do it all over again.

They were at a new modern church in Lower Hutt, which was having a series of special services to raise money for

36

missionaries still overseas and the spirits of those who'd come back. Ngaire Hobey-Kraft was there with two others and Billy had stared and stared at her. Cushla felt a bit anxious in case the lady noticed and came over to say something. Billy reckoned he'd like to be a missionary and go on trips. Cushla wondered if he really was just attracted to the excitement of the places Ngaire Hobey-Kraft had described at past services when she'd been back on furlough. She'd shown coloured slides too this time, of Ecuador and China, which looked like they were taken on another world the views were so exotic.

The service had been going on since early morning. They'd stopped for lunch and Cushla had sat outside with the boys having sandwiches and fruit fizz in the Chrysler, with all the doors open because it was so stifling. Restel had tucked in to a sit-down meal with the men. Afterwards on the lawn behind the church there'd been a lolly scramble, where one of the bigger boys got to dress up in a fancy costume, lollies in wrappers tied to it, and all the kiddies invited to chase him and grab as many lollies off the costume as they could. She was quite proud when Billy ran like the blazes and grabbed off more lollies than anyone else. She'd put them in her handbag and told Billy he'd have to share them out with his brothers when they got home. He'd grizzled a bit and so had Colin but mostly because they were fed up from the long morning sitting still and their best shorts made their legs itchy.

For the evening service, Corrie Ten Boom was going to be the guest speaker. She was on a tour of New Zealand and even Cushla was keen on seeing and hearing her, she was so famous. It was the largest service the boys had ever been to so it did keep them pretty well behaved. By late afternoon, though, Billy had fallen asleep, his head on Cushla's arm. When the snoring sound started she thought it was him and jolted him with her elbow and he slipped down to the floor just as she realized it was Colin making the noises for a dag. Billy got such a fright he yelled out 'Blinking heck!' right in the middle of their dad talking on and on about the wages of sin. Everyone looked round and Cushla went scarlet she was so embarrassed. Restel glared at her when he'd finished. He wouldn't see the funny side when they stopped for tea and he'd come over for a bit. Her and the boys had a heck of a laugh, though. Cushla laughed so much her eyes watered which always set the boys to slinging off when they saw it. Lucky for her Restel was somewhere out the back on the grass section by then, helping to cook sausages and chops, so he didn't see them laughing. And she was supposed to bear witness tonight. How the heck would she be able to?

Yet with the boys so tired and quietened down as the evening came and wore on and the emotion and singing in the church and with Bulla who'd arrived sitting with her, Cushla felt the burden of her sinning, reckoned she felt the spirit of the Lord moving within her. She joined in the hymns with fervour, sat riveted listening to Corrie Ten Boom and a special singer who sang spirituals so beautifully Cushla broke down, wept from the joy. She got to her feet almost before anyone else and marched along the aisle to the front to be blessed with Christ's redemption. Restel was sitting over with the men, beaming all across his face and nodding his head. He looked quite choked up when Billy left his seat and came out, goaded on by Bulla, to stand beside his mum holding her hand as the verses of 'Just as I am' were sung in reverent harmony before the close of the day.

All the way home in the car, Aunt Bulla sitting up in the back seat with Colin and Seddon, pleased as punch over Cushla bearing witness, talking away non-stop, Billy kept saying, 'That was the best church service I've ever been to. I've been saved now, can I have a bike?' whenever Bulla stopped for breath.

'You're not saved yet,' Colin told Billy, whispering. 'You're not old enough.'

Restel kept patting Cushla on the arm and telling her,

'You'll be rewarded in heaven, Cushla. In my father's house there are many mansions', as they careered along the road back to Upper Hutt. Bulla was planning to spend the night instead of going home alone.

The following day after they'd returned from usual Sunday church service and finished lunch, they took Bulla for a drive, up the bush, had a cup of tea beside the winding road while Restel took photographs and they all listened out for bellbirds. Seddon was dead certain he saw a kiwi running for cover but Aunt Bulla thought not.

'Most of them are gone now,' she said. 'God's feathered friends knocked off. It's shocking. When I was a girl just after we came from the Old Country, kiwis were running about all over the place. We even had one living in our yard, didn't we, Restel?'

While Bulla took a nap in the back seat of the Chrysler Restel and Cushla took the boys further into the bushland on a nature ramble, looking at the huge pongas and ferns and wild flowers. They came across a small icy-cold stream and had a paddle, laughing fit to bust when Billy fell in and got all his clothes wet. He started to shiver and bawl his eyes out so Cushla took him back to the car, holding his hand, while Restel and the others took the longer path which went in a complete circle and ended up near where the car was parked. On their way back Cushla and Billy saw a tui and then three wood pigeons, which Billy skited about for hours as the others hadn't seen anything good.

Restel gave Cushla quite a shock a few weeks later, when he told her what he had been planning for them. She'd had an idea that something was going on but wasn't sure what, or if it was anything at all, but he'd had some letters

39

through the post she'd wondered about, been quite tempted to open.

He'd been writing off about some advertisements he'd seen in the *Herald*, he told Cushla, about farming up north in the Waikato. They were crying out for people to go sharemilking.

'We're not farming people!' Cushla cried, getting into a bit of a panic.

'There's not much to learn, they train you,' Restel informed her. 'At least, these people will,' and he showed her a letter he'd had from some people on a farm near Te Aroha who were more or less offering him and his family a place on a dairy farm which had about two hundred cows. All Restel'd have to do was learn the twice-daily milking, as it was all done with machines. The idea was to enable the owners to start growing crops and expanding their land which needed bush clearance. The work wouldn't be hard. A house would be provided and there was a pretty good school nearby.

'What about Seddon's job?' Cushla asked. 'We can't just pack up and disrupt that!'

'There'll be work on the farm,' Restel said, his face going a bit pink. 'Or there'll be something else in Te Aroha. We're meant to go, Cushla. I feel the Lord wants us to. It'll be healthier. Living here is not a good influence on the boys.'

They talked about it for three days but Restel had made up his mind. He'd already written back and told them he was accepting their offer so Cushla knew her feeling windy about the whole thing was pointless. They were going. She began to dread having to tell the boys. Restel said he'd leave it up to her, she was better at things like that.

'What about money?' she suddenly asked him in bed one night. She found herself often waking up and thinking of more worries. 'We've no savings, have we? How can we afford to shift everything up there, eh? Tell me that one.'

Restel was quiet for a minute then told her, 'Bulla's

made me a loan. I told you she had a bit tucked away. She was keen to help, Cushla. She loves the boys as much as we do and worries for them. She frets for their future.'

Cushla was stunned. She was so shook that sleep didn't come at all that night, not even towards dawn when she often got off. She was furious with Bulla and brooded over the news for days.

'He's determined to go, sister,' Bulla said when Cushla tried to have it out with her. 'I couldn't have stopped him if I'd tried. I've made him the loan to make sure it all goes right. You know how he is, doing things on the cheap. I've made sure you and the boys don't go short. I'm sorry if I got your ire up. I shall miss you, Cushla, you and your dear boys. I'll be quite cut off . . .'

Her small mouth puckered and she turned away, fumbling for a hanky. Cushla found herself comforting her, there in the kitchen. Later Cushla discovered envelopes on the boys' beds, with a pound note in each. 'For the trip up, buy some lollies' Bulla had written on the envelopes.

Billy and Colin took the news quite well, and within a few days grew so excited and nervy she hardly knew what to do with them when they got home from school. The questions they asked! 'Will we have to milk cows up there?' and 'Can we go and buy some gumboots at the shops? Seddon said there'll be cowpoop all over the place.'

They had no worries about leaving school. Billy must have reckoned they were going straight away. Cushla found him packing his few books into a box he'd found out in the washhouse, panting and puffing and muttering 'Struth' over and over again. She'd had a laugh over that and explained they would not be going for a bit yet.

Seddon went into a real paddy when she told him, away from his brothers. He stomped about the house for days and wouldn't talk and would go out back slamming the door. One evening he was out there tinkering with his bike on the concrete by the shed when Restel came home from work.

Restel often seemed not to know how to talk to the boys and when he did it was with an awkwardness Cushla hadn't noticed in him at any other time. She watched him pointing out things to Seddon about his bike, and they examined the chain for a while, Restel having rolled up his sleeves and kneeling down on the concrete. Cushla sometimes felt a bit jittery when she saw any of the boys with Restel. It wasn't real jealousy but something akin to it. She didn't like the feeling, as if the boys would start spending more time with their dad if he gave them extra attention. Yet privately she wondered what on earth she would do without them, without all of them, Restel included, which made that other, jittery feeling go away.

For the next few weeks after that neither Cushla nor Restel had time for much of anything except organizing the shift. Restel handed in his notice at work and told her that they'd seemed quite relieved. He reckoned he wouldn't have been in the job much longer anyway as they were still laying men off left, right and centre.

Seddon arranged to carry on working right up to the last minute so they'd had to rely on Colin and Billy to help with all the packing, which wasn't too good as they started to get on each other's nerves. Kim, their usually absent cat, would stay behind. He was pretty old now and the shift might be too much. He still seemed stuck on Mrs Whiti next door so that solved that. Most of the furniture was going by lorry, and they began packing the rest into the trailer which the Chrysler would pull. Most families did that. People shifted all over the country, for work.

As another family with young kiddies would be moving into the house Cushla spent days having a good spring clean and sorting out rubbish in the garden. One of the nosey neighbours called out one morning, 'On the move again, are you?' as Cushla was piling bags of old newspapers out to the verge for the Thursday-morning collection. Cushla ignored her but the words shook her a bit. It was second nature to her now, shifting. Restel had moved them so many times she hated to think about it. Perhaps this shift would be the last.

Bulla kept away during all the upheaval. Restel said she'd been feeling a bit crook with arthritis and he didn't want her mucking in like she would if she was given the chance, though Cushla thought it could be because she was upset at their going. Bulla wouldn't be able to get up to where they'd be very much, if at all, as the trip'd probably be too much for her. Cushla did feel for her. She didn't have time towards the end to stop and think how she herself felt about going. If she had she would have just sat down and given up. Luckily, Seddon had eventually come round: he now mucked in and helped out in the evenings. Restel seemed pretty calm but underneath she felt his impatience over their getting off, willing the day to arrive.

'We're like blinking gypsies,' Seddon said to Cushla. 'Boy, where will we all end up, in Aussie?' and he laughed, giving her a hand with the washing-up, something he rarely did. He began sorting out the back shed with his dad, giving the Chrysler a good checking over and a spruce up ready for the big day. He hosed down and scrubbed the tarpaulin cover, changed the car oil, brought home and put in brand new spark plugs and a fan belt. Restel was as pleased as punch with him and gave him ten shillings. Seddon immediately went out and bought cakes of chocolate with some of the money and shared them with Billy and Colin.

A few nights before they were to leave Cushla was washing clothes in the copper boiler out the back. Restel

43

had driven over to Bulla's with a box of preserves Cushla didn't want to take with them. Colin had gone too, for company. Seddon was in his room studying his motor manual, as usual with Billy, who had unpacked all his books and begun to wrap them in newspapers 'so they won't get bumped on the trip, Mum,' he'd told Cushla. Cushla had taken a pile of washing out to the line and when she went back the copper had overflowed onto the floor. Sudsy water was running everywhere even after she'd turned off the taps. It was her own fault, she thought. She was too worn out, fretting too much, forgetting to turn the taps off. She went into the house to fetch Seddon to help.

The two boys were kneeling naked on the floor in front of Seddon's bed. Billy was giggling, Seddon pink-faced. The door had been shut, so on Cushla opening it the boys pulled apart, but not before Cushla saw Billy's hand on Seddon's penis. It didn't register in her mind immediately; she just knew that something was a bit wrong. Each of them became still for a long silent minute, until Cushla, beginning to understand, moved straight across the room to Billy and with her fist belted him over the side of his head so that he was knocked against the bed. She didn't touch Seddon, couldn't look at him. Unable to say a word, she left the room and returned to the washhouse, attempting to clear up the flood. Long before she'd finished she rushed to stand at the door, peering out into the darkness, her face screwed up in pain.

The morning was overcast and windy when they finally left. The lorry had gone on ahead, piled up to its roof. Seddon got permission from Restel to travel with the driver up front in the cab. Cushla hadn't bothered to argue, she was so worn out. It only took old Mrs Whiti to come out to say hooray with Kim at her feet, her giving Cushla a posy of African violets, for Cushla to break down and weep, holding Mrs Whiti in a long embrace. Restel was in a cheery mood and shook Mrs Whiti's hand, even stroked Kim who was busy patting a stinkbug on the pavement with his paw.

Colin and Billy sat in the back seat, strangely quiet. Restel kept glancing at them in the rear-vision mirror. Cushla sat very still, her handbag on her lap. They were driving over to say hooray to Bulla before starting on the trip. The car was so loaded down with the trailer as well that Restel drove more slowly than he normally did.

Cushla could not stop brooding over what she had seen Seddon and Billy doing. It shook her that she had belted Billy instead of Seddon, who was, after all, the eldest. She hadn't told Restel, wouldn't have known how the heck to explain.

Across the ranges cloud was heavy with threatened rain. The air was close, the sky a strange purple colour. In the distance towards Wellington, thunder sounded, although the weather report in the morning newspaper had reckoned there were blue skies and lots of sunshine up ahead.

Part Two

Is there a chance
that this heart inside me
is a different shape
to other people's?
Is it bigger or smaller –
Does its beat play a different
music?

Billy Bevan

On the Land with Gumboots and Cows

Cushla dipped her fingers in the pail of warm milk and pushed them upward towards the calf's mouth. Its saliva dribbled down her wrist but she carried on the way she'd been shown, the calf looking up at her with vacuous eyes. There were three of them, abandoned by their mums. Restel had suggested she look after them and teach them to drink milk from a pail rather than from a bottle. They were tethered out the back. Cushla hated the job but felt sorry for the lost little tykes. The smallest one seemed unable to grasp the idea of sucking up the milk itself and was quite content to carry on sucking it off her fingers. It was very thin and she hoped it wouldn't die. She knew nothing about cows. Restel reckoned it'd survive but how the heck he knew that when he was almost as ignorant as her, Cushla couldn't credit. He was hardly ever at the house these days. Always off somewhere in the paddocks doing extra work for the owners. She realized he was trying real hard so that he could keep the job and they could stay on. He was on a trial period, the owners had told him, while they got to know him and he could get the hang of things.

They had settled in on the farm pretty well, though Cushla reckoned it was too cut off and her being on her own most of the day was getting on her goat. Her chestiness seemed to have come back too and she wasn't sleeping well most nights. Some days she privately

49

wondered if Restel wasn't a bit mental having dragged them here. It all seemed a real dag to the boys but Cushla worried herself sick that Restel hadn't known what he was letting them in for. He appeared to have no worries for a while and clomped off long before dawn in his gumboots and oilskin and she wouldn't see him until lunchtime, and then not every day, and she was sick to death of getting a meal ready and watching it grow cold on top of the stove.

The house they'd been given was large, sprawling and run down. Most of the paint was peeling away from the weatherboards but the tiled roof looked good, much more flash than the corrugated-iron roof of the house in Upper Hutt. The Chrysler had played up quite a bit since the trip. Seddon had tinkered with it until it was going like a bomb. They really needed the car now. The nearest church was at Te Aroha, a good few miles away. The owners of the farm didn't go to church at all and Cushla noticed that Restel had kept a bit quiet about his faith. He said the owners were heavy boozers and swore a lot but were good sorts. They'd certainly been given a friendly welcome. A big get-together was being planned using the paddock out the back, so they could meet other local farmers. That was important, both Restel and Cushla had been told. Nothing much had been mentioned about the Bevans being strict Christians, although Restel had made it plain that he needed time off on Sundays to go to church. Mr Young the owner hadn't been too keen but didn't moan about it, so that was all right.

The boys had a bedroom each and there was a spare room built onto the washhouse, which Cushla wouldn't have minded using as a sewing room. They'd put her treadle Singer in there already. The room had bunk beds attached to the walls. Along with good rugs on the polished wooden floors and curtains, the people who'd been in the house before had left quite a lot of furniture all over. It was a bit cluttered with their own things as well.

50

There was a huge back yard and to the left of the hedge which surrounded it was an area of bush with a stream running through. In the early mornings while Cushla sat in the kitchen with the back door wide open, she could hear the gurgling water and the breeze through the trees. The sounds comforted her. The days in Wellington were long gone, now a memory.

After they'd settled, Seddon had found a new apprenticeship almost straight away, at a huge garage over in Morrinsville. He used his bike to get there and didn't seem too shook about the change. Colin and Billy went to a school in Te Aroha. A school bus picked them up outside the house every morning. Cushla missed them not coming home sometimes for lunch, so the days were long. She spent a lot of the time clearing the neglected vegie garden of weeds and rehanging curtains and washing windows. The work wore her out so she slept a little better at night.

Restel was keen on things at first but eventually became pretty quiet and wouldn't talk to her about his days. He came back at dusk looking aged with tiredness. Sometimes he was too weary to attend the mid-week prayer meeting and it was playing on his mind, that she could tell. They'd all been going together in the Chrysler every Sunday morning and evening to the church at Te Aroha. The boys attended Bible class and Sunday school but Restel began to worry that they were slipping away, backsliding because of the demands of his job. Cushla did her block when he'd had a moan to her about it.

'The Lord should come first, Cushla,' he'd said one night as they lay in bed. 'We made a promise to follow His path. The Youngs are not Christian people and the other men are all very impudent. I don't know what I shall do. I'll pray for guidance.'

'For goodness' sake!' Cushla almost shouted. 'You brought us here, all this way, saying how better it'd be. I didn't want to come. Look at the boys, disrupting their learning and Seddon only just starting out. Is the job too much for you, is that it, eh?'

51

'I don't like the way the other men sling off,' Restel told her. 'There's a lot of blaspheming. They have beer in the milk sheds.'

'You can't expect it to be any different than that!' Cushla snapped. 'These are farming people. I told you we weren't farmers. Haven't you got any gumption?'

They said no more, lay silently in their bed. Cushla felt herself shaking with a temper she'd rarely felt before. She'd always respected Restel's wishes but the temper had been simmering inside her ever since they'd arrived. She'd have to watch it, as she knew it was wrong, it was sinful. Restel was the head of the house, after all. She had to support him. Silently she reached out to him there in the dark, but he turned away, pulling the bedclothes over his head.

'Restel?' she whispered. 'Restel?'

Billy spent a lot of time after school on his own, once he'd come back on the bus. Although the school was smaller than the one in Upper Hutt, Colin would have even less to do with him there and now ignored him at home too. Colin had made some cobbers at the school straight away, got into a sort of gang. Billy took to watching the gang at playtime, kicking a footy ball about or climbing the jungle gym and having secret meetings behind the bike sheds. He'd tried to join in but was told he was a bit young and too much of a sissy. As the school had a library Billy often escaped there and sat reading. The library had *Famous Five* books as well as *Secret Seven* stories so there was a heck of a lot to read. The teacher didn't like him staying inside so much but allowed him to take out a book and sit under the kowhai trees, which she said was more healthy.

At the farmhouse at weekends it was different. Seddon spent a lot of time with Billy and allowed him to help clean his bike, gave him rides on the crossbar along the road after. Seddon even promised to give him a ride all the way to Morrinsville and show him where he worked at the garage.

'Boy, that'd be good,' Billy said. 'They've got two picture houses at Morrinsville. Can we go to the pictures there, Seddon? Do you reckon Mum'd let us?'

'Dunno,' said Seddon. 'I could take you, one Saturday, I suppose. You've got to promise not to say. I think Dad was pretty riled about Mum taking you that other time.'

'Why can't we go a lot?' Billy asked.

Seddon shrugged. 'Dad doesn't believe it's good for you,' he answered.

With his mate Melvin, Seddon sometimes went off rabbit shooting on the farm. Melvin's dad owned a chook farm further off in another area and Seddon was given the loan of an air rifle. He told Billy he'd take him over into the bush on the other side of the farm one day after work, just the two of them, to have a shoot at rabbits. Billy wasn't too keen about the shooting but reckoned he'd like to go anyway.

Seddon had played the game with Billy a few times in the bush out back, despite their mum having caught them at it before the shift. She hadn't said a word to Seddon but he'd been scared stiff she'd tell his dad. Seddon seemed fascinated by Billy, when the two of them were alone. Billy was not to know that it was a phase Seddon was going through. The game had become such a dag. Billy certainly liked the attention. He still couldn't figure out the hang of why Seddon wanted to play such a game with him but thought he understood the secrecy. Their mum and dad would get too het up like when his mum had found them. Her face had been real wild.

Billy didn't seem able to make any friends at the new school. They were all very big boys in his class and although he wasn't bullied much and he thought they were a bit of all right, they shied away from him outside the classroom, wouldn't let him join in their games. Just as Colin wouldn't let him join the gang he belonged to. So the game with Seddon, which was very secret and where he was expected to do rude things, became more and more his only way of feeling he was liked. His mum acted a bit funny now, when she was alone with him. She didn't hug him much, and tried to keep him away from his dad. She'd stopped telling him he was her special boy. He still reckoned he must be, and sometimes skited about it to his brothers but only to get their attention. Seddon left him alone a lot of the time and would work on the Chrysler or tinker with Melvin's souped-up Austin when Melvin came over in it. When Seddon's mate was there, Seddon ignored Billy totally. Billy would wander off onto the farm, climb over fences and explore the bush, make dams along the stream or play with the three orphan calves Cushla looked after. Mostly, though, he read his books. One Saturday morning when Melvin was out the back, Billy fetched his *Famous Five* books and showed them to Melvin. He had three now.

'They're real good,' he said, holding them up. 'Would you like to have a loan of one?'

'Don't read much,' Melvin said gruffly, staring at Billy without a grin. 'Books are for sissies.'

Seddon laughed at that but came over and ruffled Billy's hair. 'Saturday after next, or the one after,' he said quietly to Billy, and gave him a big wink, 'I'll take you to the pictures, eh?'

As Seddon spoke, Billy watched Melvin staring. On Melvin's face was a look Billy shivered at. Then Seddon, Colin and Melvin went off in Melvin's car, grinning from ear to ear. They roared up and down the road outside, kept stopping and fiddling with the engine. Billy decided to sit on the front porch to watch. He'd put his books back and took the smallest calf with him to the porch, a piece of rope tied round its neck. It kept making an awful racket and Cushla came out and blew her top at him and in the commotion the calf pooped all over the porch steps. Billy was given a hiding and made to stay in his room until tea.

Restel had begun to notice a few things about Billy he didn't care for. He reckoned Cushla had in the past fussed over him far too much, let him get away with things the other two didn't. Restel feared having a sissy for a son, as he'd often feared it in himself. Seddon and Colin were coming along nicely, already interested in manly pursuits like footy and cars and now shooting which he wasn't certain about as it was killing the Lord's creatures. Billy liked books a great deal, which wasn't a bad thing, but he had no interest in sport at all and stuck close to his mum far too much, and the books he did read weren't healthy. Yet Restel's new job on the farm was so demanding there was little time for him to do anything about it. He was still shook over finding Billy in the bathroom that time, had wondered how the heck he could have known what he was doing, or if he had known at all, rubbing himself like that. It had shocked Restel, hurt him deeply. He'd even written to Bulla about it, unable to speak to Cushla. Bulla had also been shocked, but more at Restel having the nerve to bring the subject up, which just wasn't done by good Christian people. She had written little in return to Restel about it, except that he should keep an eye on Billy and look to the day when Billy got saved, properly, which would stop any nonsense. Restel had in the past left most of the discipline to Cushla, as in that area he felt lost, unable to understand his sons as his own, part of his flesh and his heart. It was better to say nothing perhaps, and let the Lord watch over them. Yet it might do no harm to give Billy some good hard beatings. He needed knocks like that if he was going to grow up to be a real man.

*

Mr Young the farm owner had constructed a brick cooker in the back paddock, beyond the hedge, far enough away from the bush not to create a fire risk. Fire was dreaded on the farm, during the long scorching summers. The brick cooker was temporary, ready for the gathering he'd planned. Quite a number of the other sharemilkers in the area had been asked to come, with their wives and girlfriends, as he wanted the Bevans to feel at home and couldn't yet feel that they did. It'd been a risk taking on an inexperienced milker but in New Zealand a job was a job and who was he to stop a good keen bloke from having a go. Restel Bevan certainly was keen, he'd give him credit for that.

'Good day, Mrs Bevan!' he called out as he was clearing the dry grass from round the cooker. 'How're doing, eh?'

'All right, Mr Young, thank you,' Cushla replied, and gave him a smile. She was hanging out the washing on the new line Restel had put up in the back yard. Cushla never knew what to say to Mr Young. He was quite different from Restel, tall and broad with a handsome, weather-tanned face. He was always friendly and seemed sincere, but Restel expected her to avoid getting too friendly with people who weren't Christian. Mr Young confused her as Cushla couldn't ignore his friendliness. He was their boss. She saw a great deal of him about the place, digging holes for fence posts and checking with her a lot to see if she needed anything for the house. It all seemed a bit too good to be true, that. It made her a bit embarrassed. Cushla smiled at Mr Young again before carrying the wooden wash-box indoors. The house had a second-hand electric washer and she was still getting the hang of it. She'd already almost caught her fingers in the wringer a couple of times. She wasn't certain she liked it after years with a copper boiler.

Cushla was quite looking forward to the get-together Mr Young was planning. She hadn't met any other farmers yet, although they seemed to have been here for ages. There were no other church people living nearby. Some of them from the Te Aroha church were planning to drive over but most lived too far away and petrol was expensive.

On the day the get-together was to take place Restel made the boys stay close to the house. Restel had been given the day off. It was the first time in weeks that they'd all been together. Cushla was up before dawn, cooking girdle scones on the stove and making fruit salad and buttering bread. The get-together was to be a combined effort but Cushla was determined to offer a lot of food so no one would think they were skinflints. Restel told her that Mr Young was providing most of the refreshments but not what they'd be. Restel was acting a bit queer about today. He hadn't told her how many were coming or who they were, when she was certain he knew. He just kept saying it'd been all Mr Young's idea and he was only one sharemilker amongst several employed by him on farms all over the area.

Billy, as she'd reckoned he would, came rushing into the kitchen still half-asleep, in his pyjamas, before the others had even stirred. She'd left Restel to have a lie in.

'Can I butter some scones?' Billy asked.

'They aren't ready yet, son. Tell you what, go and get a pail of milk from the sheds and you can give the calves a feed.'

'Oh yeah, I'd like that,' Billy shouted.

Cushla told him to shoosh and to get his clothes on first and an oilskin as it was drizzling outside.

Cushla felt rather crook this morning. She had lain awake most of the long night, just unable to sleep. Cushla had no one she could talk to here, she felt so cut off. Because of Restel's wandering she had removed herself from the closeness of her brother and sister and now they were both as good as dead. She never saw them. They hated writing letters. She'd had a note from Radley a while back, just to say he was all right. Being here on this farm miles away from Wellington, Cushla felt like a fish out of water. Restel never came home except to eat and sleep and drive them to church where they'd got to know no one properly. It all whirled about like a hot wind, thoughts of regret about her marriage causing her heart to ache, only held at bay because of that special love she had for Billy. She loved Colin and Seddon too, yet Billy, Billy with his odd little ways and his differences and his bright shining face, she loved Billy desperately. Yet strange feelings were beginning to form like shadows, there inside her, when she looked at him. He was too different from his brothers.

Towards late afternoon people began to turn up for the get-together. They arrived on motorbikes and on foot and hanging on the back of trucks. There were Maori blokes in black singlets and shorts and women carrying boxes of food and kiddies running. Cushla was pretty put out. She'd no idea there'd be so many. Billy sat with Colin and Seddon on the front porch, quite flabbergasted at all the noise and the laughter and people calling out, 'Good day, you jokers, where's the bloody tucker being cooked, eh?' with cries of welcome between couples who hadn't seen one another for weeks. All of them moving down the side of the house towards the paddock out the back. Most of them carried blankets and folding-chairs and crates of drinks.

'Blimey,' Seddon kept saying, 'they must have come for a week!'

Restel stood just inside the front door, which was propped open to allow a breeze to cool the house. His face began to grow red as the crowd arrived and he noticed all the crates of beer.

Cushla stayed in the kitchen once she'd seen the

58

number of people. The amount of noise being made threatened to deepen her mood of the morning but she busied herself getting food together and ginger-beer cordial Restel had made up. The recipe had been Bulla's. They all loved it but it wouldn't go far, not with this crowd. She watched them through the back window as they clomped across the yard, through the gap in the hedge to where Mr Young stood with his wife Lynette. They all look so rough, she thought. Shouting and laughing and the men slapping each other on their backs and the women all wearing make-up and lipstick and stockings. When she saw the beer bottles being opened and even the women drinking from them and one bloke with his hand on another bloke's wife's bottom, squeezing it and laughing like mad, she put a hand up to cover her mouth. Stood there with an awful feeling, that this might be a real mistake being here in this cow country, becoming sharper as more people arrived and the raucous laughter grew louder and the beer flowed.

Dying in the Night

The get-together had gone on all day, then for half the night, though without the Bevans. Two of the share-milkers had a dingdong fist fight over someone else's wife but it was all sorted out and the men left having shook hands and apologized to each other. Very early on Cushla had got the boys to take out the buttered scones and the fruit salad and the ginger-beer cordial. Most of the cordial hadn't been touched except for a few of the smaller kiddies having some and several of the women trying it. Mr Young and Lynette had spent their time cooking sausages and steaks on the cooker, handing them out on tin plates. Bowls of salad were set out on trestle tables for everyone to help themselves. Despite her apprehension, Cushla changed into her best frock, tidied her hair and went out to say 'hello' to Mr Young, and to Lynette whom she'd never met. She called Lynette 'Mrs Young' and several people round began to laugh and Mr Young went a bit pink. Cushla was told they weren't married but just lived together. She hadn't known what to say, looking back to the house for Restel. Before she knew it, she was standing there holding an opened bottle of beer someone handed her and Restel was staring at her across the hedge from where he stood in the yard. Cushla became flustered and dropped the bottle. Some of the beer frothed up and splashed her legs. She was still able to smell the pong hours later.

They'd all been a heck of a friendly lot. So many had come up and introduced themselves to Cushla, she forgot each new name as soon as she'd heard it. She stood there beside Lynette in a welter of embarrassment, unable to move away, grinning so much her jaw began to ache. Around her stood hulking hairy-chested blokes in singlets and shorts, many with gumboots on who laughed and joked and flirted with the other women, and her, until the faces seemed to mould into one huge leering grin. She must have acted a bit crook as suddenly she was sitting on a wooden form with two women, one of whom kept patting her arm and fanning her face and trying to encourage her to have a sip of beer. One woman told her she had such gorgeous auburn hair and a perfect figure. All Cushla could feel was panic.

Seddon, Colin and Billy mingled with the others immediately, Colin and Billy tearing round the paddock playing some sort of chasing game with the other kiddies while Seddon moved over to stand near the men, watching them in a fascination so obvious he was soon being offered beer too, which he drank with constant red-faced, shifty glances to where his mum was sitting. Restel flatly refused to join Cushla, had gone back inside the house, his face, like Seddon's, quite scarlet, though for different reasons. He left Cushla to fend for herself but after a while, when her panic had subsided, she sat with a glass of ginger-beer cordial and chatted away to the other women who'd flocked round. The talk was a bit lewd yet they shared recipe ideas and most of the women tried out the ginger-beer and wanted a copy of the recipe, they said it was so scrumptious. Cushla envied them their real relaxed ways and felt so dowdy. She was the only wife there without make-up or stockings. A few of the women smoked cigarettes, holding them level with their faces, their arms turned back, posing for the men a short distance away, casting them openly flirting looks. The men were such handsome, healthy-looking brutes Cushla could not help looking over at them herself from time to time, yet the guilt building up inside her became a tight band across her chest and her breathing, never good, became more and more wheezy. Not that anyone noticed.

She hadn't been amongst such friendly, carefree folk since she'd been a girl and her mum and dad had gathered their friends together in Wellington. Yet she felt quite unable to relax, aware of Restel's absence, trying to deal with the veiled hints some of the women were starting to make as to where he was.

Cushla had not been allowed to mix with such a group of people since Restel had married her. It shook her. At church gatherings the kiddies would be strictly organized into playing games, Pin the Tail on the Donkey or Blind Man's Buff. There would be hymn singing and readings from the Bible. Here she felt she'd been dunked into a different world, company she had been deprived of, company she'd forgotten about. The kiddies ran about all over the paddock, although they were well-behaved little tykes on the whole and didn't go beyond the hedge into the yard. The adults simply stood about boozing and tucking into the food, some sprawled in groups on the grass with the crates of beer, with the men and the women mostly in separate groups, despite all the flirting and lewd jokes and looks going back and forth. The flirting mesmerized Cushla.

Lynette came over and whispered in Cushla's ear. 'Mr Young's a bit worried about your husband, Mrs Bevan. Is he all right?'

Cushla stared at her for a minute, at a loss as to what to say in reply.

'He's been pretty tired lately, Mrs . . . um, Lynette. I'll go and see if he's all right. I've more scones in the kitchen. The others have been all snapped up!' and she grinned as well as she could, wondering what on earth Restel would say when she went indoors.

'Mum, Mum, can I show my room off?' Billy began shouting at her as she headed towards the house. His face was flushed and his eyes sparkled as he looked over at her. He was surrounded by other kiddies, she'd never seen him so excited and happy. Her heart went out to him. Seeing her expression he came over and held her hand, looking up into her face.

'Where's Dad?' he asked.

'I think he's feeling a bit crook, son,' Cushla replied.

'Don't suppose he likes all the beer. I didn't drink any, Mum. Seddon's drunk some. I was good,' he told her, walking across the back yard with her to the door, which was shut. Cushla glanced at the calves. They seemed quiet enough and she realized she hadn't given them an afternoon feed. Because of what followed she forgot.

After organizing Billy into taking another tray of scones out, she waited until he'd gone before calling out to Restel. There was only silence in return.

She found him in their bedroom. He was sitting on the edge of the bed, his Bible lying open across his lap, staring out through the window at the parked cars on the road. His face was now pasty-white. He wouldn't look at her as she said quietly, 'Restel?' at the doorway, unable to enter. She stood there for quite a while, hating the heavy silence, staring at his profile. He had lowered his sight and appeared to be reading, his lips moving slightly and his hands white at the knuckles.

'I'm sorry, Restel,' she said finally. 'I wasn't to know it'd be like this. You weren't to know, either. I'm keeping an eye on the boys but I reckon you should be out there. Lynette was a bit worried you'd been taken crook.'

Restel looked up at her then, and Cushla could see fear in his eyes. 'I don't know what you think you're doing,' he said quietly. 'You know how I feel about drinking and lewd behaviour. I want you to bring the boys indoors. I won't have them exposed to it!'

'What the heck am I supposed to say to Mr Young?' Cushla snapped. 'There they are being real friendly, they're asking where you are! They aren't all drinking beer. They're good people, Restel, good sorts. You said so yourself after we got here. Mr Young wants us to feel part of it.'

'I will not have any sinning in this house, Cushla,' Restel told her. 'You're forgetting whose path we've chosen to follow.'

'Oh, for goodness' sake. Do you want to lose this job? Just like all the others?' Cushla almost shouted at him.

At that moment there was a terrific commotion from the back door. Cushla could hear Billy's voice above the din. She looked out into the hall. Billy was herding dozens of kiddies into his room. They were all giggling and pushing at each other to be first.

'I've got lots of books and stuff!' he was yelling above all the other kiddies' voices. It was bedlam. From outside now a voice was calling her.

'Mrs Bevan, are you there? Can I pinch some water and rags? My bloody kids have chucked up all over the place!'

It was one of the Maori mothers Cushla had chatted to. Through the kitchen window as she craned her neck, she could see a bunch of people standing about in the yard near the steps. Kiddies were still piling through the door into Billy's room, clambering over each other and screeching with laughter. Cushla took one more look at Restel then left the room. He had returned to staring out at the road, had moved so his back was to the door. Cushla shut it before she went out back, grinning. Her face was bright red.

The get-together grew steadily rowdier as the afternoon moved into early evening. Cushla tried her best to be cheery and polite but as tiredness reached towards her she slowly grew more tense and nervy. Restel did appear, clomping off towards the milking sheds in his work clothes, not even looking in her direction. The women seemed to have gathered there was something wrong but by now a lot of them were acting pretty drunk and more beer had arrived, on the back of one of the trucks. A group of Maoris had got together and were singing. Cushla sat listening, enthralled at the beauty of it. She had no idea where the boys had gone off to. She hadn't seen them for hours. It was almost dark when Restel appeared again. He was dragging Seddon by the arm. Seddon was falling about all over the place, laughing fit to bust, his shirt halfway out of his pants and his hair a mess. Cushla got to her feet and ran to them. Restel's face was more angry than she'd seen it for ages.

'He's drunk, Cushla. He's been drinking beer down behind the sheds. He reeks of it. Where's Colin and Billy?'

Cushla shook her head, unable to answer, took Seddon's arm as Restel let the boy go and he threatened to fall down. Restel, after one stricken look at her, hurried into the house. As she helped Seddon up the steps, he started shouting out at the top of his voice, slurring the words, 'Full as a bull's bum, Mum!' over and over again. Then Restel came striding back out, his Bible in his hand, moving purposefully past her, almost knocking her over, heading towards the revelry in the paddock. Cushla froze for a long minute, her heart thudding, helping Seddon inside to his room, trying not to think about what Restel would say to the folks out there. Panic returning with a rush, trying to keep Seddon sitting up straight as she undressed him and got him into bed, shooshing him as he began to sing a song with what she reckoned were filthy words. As soon as he lay down and she'd pulled the blankets over him he threw up, all over her arms and the sheet, beginning to groan and kick his legs out. Cushla let go of him, stood there and started to weep from the tension inside her, holding her hands up to her face then realizing they were covered with sick. After a few minutes she pulled off Seddon's bedding, covering him with a clean blanket before going to have a good wash in the bathroom.

She returned to the kitchen when the sound of shouting reached her. Seddon had quietened, falling into a deep sleep. From the window she could make out Restel standing facing Mr Young and Lynette watched by the others, who had mostly fallen silent. No one was laughing. It was Restel doing the shouting. He was waving his Bible in the air and gesticulating wildly. Cushla backed away from the window.

When Restel came indoors, dragging Colin and Billy with him, Billy bawling his eyes out and both of them dishevelled, Cushla was sitting at the table with a cup of tea. She hadn't been able to face going back out there again. Restel sent Billy and Colin straight to their rooms after clouting them across the head, went too, after standing there for a minute, closing their bedroom door after him without once having looked at Cushla nor spoken to her. Outside, the noise had got back to what it had been before, laughter and shouts and singing with more and more people now arriving. There was music playing, blokes dancing with their wives, and no one near the yard. Coloured lights had been strung up along the top of the hedge, and as the darkness fell the hues of the lights entered the kitchen, touching Cushla's face as she sat unmoving, her breathing loud in the room. The darkness, combined with the soft lights, appeared to comfort her.

After a while, thinking she might take Restel a cup of tea, she had moved across to get the jug when Billy came into the kitchen, and stood there peering at her.

'Seddon's been sick all over the blinking floor, Mum,' he said. 'Boy, it sure pongs. He's moaning like mad.'

Cushla went to bed hours later, lay awake beside Restel listening to the voices and the music and the raucous laughter. Restel lay on his side, on the far side of the bed, as far away from her as he could, the bedclothes covering him completely. He had left the light on for her. On her pillow he had placed his Bible. She lay on her back terrified that she would wake him and he would begin to accuse her. Dreading the morning that eventually would arrive.

In the aftermath the following morning Billy found the smallest calf lying dead on the frost-covered grass. He was up before anyone else, even his mum. None of them had got much sleep. Abandoned across the grass and beyond the hedge in the paddock were empty beer bottles and below one of the macrocarpa trees near the edge of the bush was a bloke lying on his back, asleep. The air was chilly yet the blue sky promised another scorching day. Billy stared at the sleeping bloke then at the dead calf. He watched one of the other calves nudging at it with a snuffling nose. The calf's body was quite stiff and cold when he touched it.

'Boy, they're gunna cop it over this,' Billy said to himself.

Billy was still sitting beside the dead calf when Mr Young appeared. He took one look over the top of the hedge then came through the gap and knelt down. He gave Billy a tired grin and ruffled his hair.

'It's dead,' Billy said needlessly. 'It's as cold as mutton. Must have died in the night.'

'Can't be helped, eh,' Mr Young told him. 'It was a runt, Billy. D'you know what that is?'

'Because it was so little?'

'That's right. The others rejected it, just like its mum did. Didn't stand a chance, not with these two greedy buggers. Poor little blighter, eh.'

'Why do runts get born?' asked Billy.

Mr Young shrugged his shoulders. 'Hard to say. Bad

blood, I reckon. Some of them survive. This little bastard didn't have much pluck in him. Happens all the time. Part of the job.'

He picked up the calf by its back legs and in one movement threw it over his shoulder, standing up as he did so.

'Your dad all right?' Mr Young asked.

Billy looked up into Mr Young's face. 'I think he's still asleep. He did his block about all that boozing yesterday.'

'Oh yeah. I reckon I'll have to talk to your dad, son. Didn't think much of his ranting and raving at me in front of my mates. Bible bashing it was. A bit bloody crook, that.'

Billy felt his face going bright scarlet. He ducked his head and stared at the ground.

Mr Young said, 'You had a good time though, eh? Saw you tucking in to all the tucker, going back for more. Did you have a good time, son?'

Billy grinned and stood to his feet. 'Yes, it was beaudy, thanks.'

When Mr Young had moved out of sight across the paddocks with the dead calf, Billy fetched the milk pails from the porch, ran all the way down to the sheds and struggled back with them filled to the brim with warm milk. He sat down and fed the two remaining calves. They were starving and jostled his arms as they drank. There were still no sounds from inside the house despite the racket the calves had begun to make. It was getting a bit late and he wondered if he should wake everyone up. They would be late for morning church as it was Sunday.

Billy stared across the paddock at the bloke lying asleep. Moving round the yard he began to collect the empty beer bottles, putting them in a pile by the hedge. His eyes hardly moving away from the motionless figure on the far side, he wandered out into the paddock, still collecting the empties, hoping the clinking of the bottles might wake the bloke up. Mr Young hadn't noticed the figure. Now there was no one about when Billy looked. There didn't seem to be anyone moving around down near the sheds. He could see the cows disappearing across the top of the ridge to the paddock they normally grazed on during the morning. The sun was high now, the frost on the grass gone. Above him two hawks were hovering several miles apart.

He stood very still when he spotted the possum. It was sitting in a ponga to the left of the house. The possum was dead still too, watching Billy with its huge brown eyes, closer than he'd ever seen one before. There were so many of them round the farm but most were shot on sight. Billy sneezed loudly and when he looked up the possum was gone.

He approached the sleeping figure slowly, calling out, 'Mister, are you awake?'

There was no movement, no sound of snoring as he got closer. Hesitantly he leaned over to look at the bloke's face half-hidden by one of his arms. There was sick all down his chin and over his chest. And in his mouth, which was open. When Billy reached out and touched the bloke's forehead with his fingers, he drew back, then stumbled, falling on his bum. The figure didn't move. The skin had been cold to the touch. Like the calf, the bloke was dead.

'Oh boy,' Billy whispered.

He sat there leaning forward, staring first at the figure, then around him. The sick stunk. Blowflies had settled on the body. Seddon's sick had stunk like this, Billy thought, last night. And after his mum had gone to bed and Billy had crept back into Seddon's room, Seddon had been lying as still as this bloke and Billy couldn't remember his brother making any breathing sounds either.

Scrambling to his feet Billy turned and, not looking back, raced across the grass towards the house, yelling Seddon's name at the top of his voice.

In the Scorching Summer Sun

The bloke in the paddock had died by choking on his vomit. There was a hoo-ha over the death which dragged on for weeks. Coppers came to ask Billy questions. The area around the paddock was carefully searched in case of foul play. There was soon little doubt that the death had been caused by the bloke having drunk enough beer for him to have passed out, and sometime in the night had woken up and chucked up and that had killed him; a blockage in the throat. No one knew why he'd lain down there to sleep. No one recalled even seeing him. He'd been one of the new, single sharemilkers and few had known him well. It was a heck of a bit of bad luck, the coppers told Cushla and Restel when they'd finished asking Billy questions.

'Your boy does seem a bit shook about finding the body,' one of the coppers added. 'The joker'd been dead for hours. It wasn't a very nice sight, bloody flies all over him.'

The death, as upsetting as it had been, helped Cushla and Restel to forget the business of the get-together once time had gone by. Yet Restel confined the boys to the house and yard for a while. It drew the family inward, if not together, and relations between Restel and Mr Young became strained. Mr Young did not appear about the house and Cushla took to watching out for him, saw him sometimes off in the distance on the tractor. She would wave to him, and he'd wave back but that was all. None of the others she'd chatted to came to visit.

*

A few weeks after the hoo-ha had died down, Restel gave Billy a severe belting for no other reason than he'd refused on two nights running to help with the washing-up after tea. Since Billy had found the body of the sharemilker he'd acted cranky and very cheeky to his dad. Cushla hadn't known how to handle him. Restel shut Billy into his room for an hour, telling him he was to get a belting, then sat reading his Bible on the front porch, not speaking to Cushla nor the other boys during that time, letting Billy stew in his room with the window shut. After the hour had passed he took his leather braces, shut and locked Billy's door behind him and, while Cushla sat at the kitchen table, he belted Billy mercilessly across his bare bum and legs before reading passages from the Bible about what sin would do to the soul. Cushla did nothing to prevent the belting, sat stiffly at the table while Seddon had a go at her, causing her face to grow pale, his words shook her so much. Seddon fell silent when Billy began to scream. It brought Colin from his room to join them. They were forced to listen to Restel's angered voice, growing louder and louder when Billy's screams subsided.

Seddon ran from the kitchen and banged on Billy's door with his fists, shouting, 'Leave him alone, leave him alone!' bringing no response except for a frightening silence, in which Seddon fled from the house, Colin following. Cushla remained where she was, trying hard to hold onto the thought that Restel knew what he was doing.

She could not understand the reason Restel had suddenly belted Billy so savagely; it was like that other time in Wellington. There was no sense to his behaviour, no sense at all.

Later, when Restel was sitting alone in the living-room reading the newspaper, Cushla went in to comfort Billy. He was lying curled up on the bed, still naked from the waist down, red marks across his skin which made her wince. She fetched some salve from the bathroom and silently applied it. At least the skin hadn't been broken. It'd been the screaming that had shaken them. Restel didn't seem to have hurt Billy badly. But Cushla hated to see Billy lying there, staring out through the window to the fruit trees, his eyes puffy from crying. He pulled away at first when she touched him, with a look of terror, then, seeing who it was, he lay very still and would not look at her, yet nor did he turn his face away. Just stared through the window, outside to where the night was coming down.

As she went to leave him, he said, 'Seddon's gonna take me to the pictures and I'm going to go too on Saturday, so there.' Cushla didn't reply, just closed the door softly behind her.

The following Sunday afternoon a few church people drove over from Te Aroha bringing with them a picnic lunch. Restel had invited them. For a few hours the cloud which had hung over the house lifted and the sun peeked out. They all sat together in the yard, on the grass. Mr Young had taken the two calves away as they had begun to feed themselves. He hadn't said much about the dead runt. The peace and the lazy comfort of the cicadas and a light breeze brought an easy friendship to where they gathered. Even Restel seemed at ease. They ate sausages in batter and whitebait fritters and salad, drank some of the ginger-beer cordial and sang hymns. Two of the men prayed with the Bevans, asking for the Lord's light to shine down and give comfort. Restel had told them about the get-together. About the boozing and the swearing and the lewd behaviour. Cushla was disturbed he hadn't mentioned Seddon's being shickered nor Billy's belting, made it seem as if he, as head of the house, was in control. Seddon went scarlet, sitting there listening to his dad ranting on and on. When Colin answered questions about school it was with his slight stutter. Billy sat beside Cushla, remained close to her all the afternoon, following her inside when she went to the kitchen to fetch something, keeping as far away from his dad as he could. Somehow they gave the impression that they were a pretty tight, Christian family. But when the visitors had gone off in their cars and trucks, the cloud having hovered nearby, came back, covered them with silence and began to give Cushla cause to feel a bit windy about the future. About where they might all end up. It was only a feeling, nothing solid and she was tired. She wondered if it might just be her, worrying, wishing things to be better, a confusion inside her.

Seddon arranged to take Billy on his bike to the pictures in Morrinsville. He told Cushla on the quiet and she let on that Billy had already said.

'Don't say to Dad,' Seddon told her. 'He'll only have a moan and stop us. He shouldn't've belted Billy like that, Mum. It isn't blinking right. He's just picking on Billy because he's so small.'

Cushla hung her head and didn't say a word, though she felt like it. Before they left she told Seddon, 'He doesn't want Billy growing up to be a sissy, Seddon. That's all. He's worried sick over you boys. You think about it, son. He is your dad.'

Seddon went scarlet and slammed the back door as he went out. Colin was watching from the hall. When Cushla turned to look at him he darted back to his room. He was doing his swotting, for exams at school, and hadn't wanted to go to the pictures. Cushla told Restel, when he came home for lunch, that Seddon and Billy had gone fishing in a stream near Te Aroha. Restel stared at her. She felt her face grow hot because of the lie.

It was a long haul to the Regent Picture House in Morrinsville. Billy sat on the crossbar of the bike, which wasn't allowed on main roads but they took the risk. Seddon sweated buckets on the way, as the sun was already scorching. There was an eleven o'clock matinée for the kiddies. They were showing a brand-new picture called *Tammy* about a girl living in the sticks way out in America. There'd be an Aussie newsreel too, a cartoon, possibly a travelogue and an episode of a Lone Ranger serial. It all sounded great to Billy. Seddon was going to show Billy where he worked and where he hung about at lunchtimes. Said he'd shout Billy some lunch after as they might meet up with Seddon's mate Melvin.

Although it made his bum pretty sore, Billy liked sitting on the crossbar of Seddon's bike, close to his big brother. They stopped every so often and had a rest, Seddon with his arm round Billy's shoulders, ruffling his hair.

'Phew, it sure is hot,' Seddon said. After a few minutes he asked, 'Are you still sore from that walloping?'

'That was ages ago, Seddon. Mum put some stuff on so it's all right now. Dad's a stinker sometimes.'

Seddon grinned and pulled Billy to him. They were resting on a log beside the road. The sky was pale blue from the stifling heat and around them was that particular silence only found on country roads. Very little traffic had passed. They were well over halfway there. Behind them, the toetoe rustled though there wasn't a sign of a breeze.

'Looking forward to the pictures?' asked Seddon.

'Oh boy, yeah. Will it be dear to get in? How much is it?'

'Dunno, I've got enough. We'd better get going, Billy. Not too far now. Your bum not too numb, eh?'

Billy looked up into Seddon's face and grinned from ear to ear. 'Nah,' he said.

The picture show was about to start when they reached the theatre. Seddon left the bike with several others on the rack provided, gave money to Billy to buy lollies while he bought the tickets. Billy chose some gobstoppers, and a box of jaffas which were Seddon's favourites. When they went in through the double swing doors it was black as pitch. Billy felt for Seddon's hand and held on tight. A Movietone newsreel was just starting. It took ages for their eyes to adjust to find seats in the dark. There was no usherette. Kiddies of all ages were running up and down the middle aisle making a heck of a racket but they soon sat down after the cartoon began. Billy sat and sucked his gobstoppers, leaning against Seddon's shoulder. When Seddon shifted in his seat his box of jaffas tipped up and the lollies spilt out onto the floor. They rolled down the uncarpeted incline all the way to the front where the little kiddies in the cheap seats picked them up and yelled out, 'Ta, you jokers!' in loud giggling voices.

Billy reckoned after that he'd enjoyed the picture show far more than the one he'd seen with Mum and Colin. He even remembered the words to the big song from the film and sang them as they were herded out by the usherettes, who were all over the place by then, acting real bossy.

They were standing on the corner of Canada Street outside the Anglican church when Seddon heard Melvin yelling out to him. He looked up and down the main street but couldn't see him until a strange coloured Morris Minor roared up to the kerb and Melvin poked his head out the window.

'Struth,' Seddon said. 'Where'd you get this old bomb?'

Melvin laughed then stared at Billy. 'I just bought it off your boss at the garage,' he said.

'Oh yeah! Blimey, that wreck's been sitting out the back since I started. Didn't think it even went. Where's the Austin?'

'Um, it's at home. Why don't you hop in, we'll go for a burn-up. I've been tinkering with the motor.'

Seddon explained about the picture show and his bike and their having to get back home. They decided to go to the milk bar instead, across the road, for a drink. Melvin tied Seddon's bike to the roof rack and parked the car outside before they went in, sitting down at the tables along the back with milkshakes and buttered pikelets. A few minutes later the bloke who had served them at the counter came over. He was so big he towered over them.

'That crate yours, mate?' he asked Melvin, pointing out towards the car.

'That's right,' Melvin said. 'What's it to you?'

'Oh, no worries, mate, no worries. I was just looking at her. Thought I'd seen her before,' he said, grinning at them in a friendly way. 'That queer colour. Seems like I know that car.'

'It belonged to some family used to live down by the railway,' Melvin told him. 'You know, where that old geezer hung himself.'

Billy thought Melvin was a bit rough. He wasn't certain he liked him much. He tucked into his pikelets and said nothing. Seddon hadn't even looked at him since Melvin had turned up, and sat next to Melvin at the table, letting Billy sit on his own.

'Oh yeah, I know,' the big man was saying. 'Bird, that was their name. Queer lot, belonged to those religious nutters. Buggered if I don't remember their little boy. Used to come in here, queer little blighter. Wonder what happened to those bastards.'

After a while, the big bloke wandered back to the counter, flicking at flies with his towel.

'I've got some booze in the boot,' Melvin said when they were alone. 'How about we get sloshed, eh?'

Seddon shook his head and glanced back at Billy. 'Nah, I'd better get Billy home. Dad'll do his block if he finds out where we are, too right.'

'It's a real bastard having an old man like yours, eh,' Melvin said and burst out laughing, shoving Seddon in the shoulder.

When Melvin had gone, leaving them with the bike on the

outskirts of town, Billy asked, 'Do you like that Melvin?' and Seddon went a bit pink and stared at Billy in a strange way.

'Yeah, he's all right, why?'

Billy didn't want to say. He stayed silent.

'He's a bit rough but most farming people are,' Seddon said after a few minutes. 'He's a good mate, though. He loaned me that air rifle and that. You'll have a mate one day, Billy, don't you worry. Melvin's not bad.'

Before they started back Seddon bought a couple of meat pies and some Lemon and Paeroa for their lunch. They sat on the grass verge, their feet in the gutter, watching the world go by. Most of the shops were shut but cars and hot rods were dragging up and down the main street. There was a queue outside the Regent for the afternoon show. The cars and hot rods were chocca with young blokes with their girls, honking horns and yelling out as they sped past. Billy's eyes nearly popped out when Seddon pulled out a packet of DeReske smokes and matches, had a smoke right there where they sat.

'Does Dad know you have smokes?' Billy asked. Seddon just shrugged, then grinned at Billy.

'Heck no, use your gumption,' he said. 'The old basket'd do his block if he knew. You won't tell on me, will you, Billy?'

'Course not. I'm no tattletale. Why doesn't Dad give you beltings like he does me? He didn't when you got drunk. It's not fair.'

Seddon stared straight ahead. 'Wouldn't let him. He shouldn't do it to you either. He's been picking on you. Little squirt, I'll get him for it one day.'

They were halfway home when Seddon remembered he hadn't shown Billy the garage where he worked. Billy reckoned it was all right, it didn't matter, he'd had such a beaut time.

'Next time, eh, when we come back,' Seddon told him. 'It's been all right today, hasn't it, Billy? Just you and me. Well, Melvin for a bit,' and he took one hand off the handlebars and ruffled Billy's blond hair, tickling the back of Billy's neck which always caused Billy to giggle with pleasure. 'You're all right, Billy. I'll never feel the same about anyone as I feel about you. Dunno why, it's just been like that. I reckon it's that you nearly died when you were a baby and I can just about remember that. I'll never hurt you, Billy.'

Billy turned his head, careful to keep his balance on the crossbar of the bike, looking into Seddon's face, which had gone a deep scarlet. Seddon had never spoken to him like that before.

The hot afternoon beat down on their heads. Their hair was already bleached almost white from the summer sun and ahead of them the long straight road shimmered in the heat. On both sides areas of bush and paddocks dotted with red-roofed farmhouses spread out as far as the eyes could see. The grass there was burnt yellow. Dust hung in the air along with the blowflies. Way up in the blue two hawks hovered. To the left but further off, almost a speck, hung a third. Billy told Seddon it'd been the best day out he'd had for ages.

As Blinded Strangers

The stifling summer heat had intensified. Small fires were breaking out on the plains to the south. Smoke drifted across the sky as the weeks passed. There seemed no relief. The air was still, without breezes. A slight easing of the heat came after dark. The land became brittle and crumbling and looked older than time.

Cushla began sitting on the porch in the evenings, alone, watching the sun slip down and the cooler darkness taking over. There was a constant smell of bush fire in the air. The back yard had begun to crack as the ground dried up. There were water restrictions and continued warnings of fire.

Restel stayed away some days until long after Cushla had sat down to tea with the boys, coming home across the paddocks as dusk deepened into the night. He'd lost weight and was dark with tan, looked healthy, yet his tiredness frightened her as it brought on flashes of short temper she knew he was directing towards Billy, who went out of his way to keep distance between them. Restel had not come near Cushla, hadn't touched her for so long she began to feel as dry and parched as the yard she wasn't allowed to tend to because of water shortage. Most of the vegies and fruit were ruined. She'd bottled some, made preserves, sweating buckets in the airless kitchen. Christmas had come and gone yet she'd had no feeling for it, had set down few plans and spent most of that time remembering past years, reaching so far back into the memory of her girlhood in Wellington it helped the present fade. Chores about the house and the long nights when she lay awake through Restel's snoring became like a shadow play. Restel stared at her a lot. She realized he suspected that she'd lied about Seddon and Billy going off to the pictures – which they'd done several times now. Melvin had nearly let it out one Saturday night when he'd been there for tea and Restel was home early, eating with them at the table.

Seddon also spent a great deal of time alone with Melvin, who Cushla didn't like. Melvin was a lot older than her son, they went rabbit shooting on the farm and tinkered with Melvin's car out on the road, which both of them seemed stuck on. Of course, cars were Seddon's job. He had done well at the Morrinsville garage, had been given a raise and more responsibility and was often invited to the owner's house for tea, where he'd stay overnight. His boss was real pleased with him. Restel said little about Seddon staying out. He left Colin alone too and concentrated his attention on Billy. It shook Cushla, that. Restel watched Billy. He questioned things Billy did, gave him lectures about his lack of interest in sport, or his failure to help out on the farm as Colin and Seddon often did on Saturday afternoons, digging trenches and clearing scrub. They appeared to enjoy doing the work, while Billy would often disappear into the bush with his books. Cushla found some notebooks beneath the bed in his room, with strange little poems written in them in his neat hand. A couple of them made Cushla get quite teary.

Restel seemed to look for any excuse to give Billy a belting. Cushla almost shouted at him about it.

'You'll make him crook!' she said one evening. 'It isn't right, Restel; you have no right to belt him when Seddon and Colin get away with things. Where's your gumption, where's the good?'

'He needs toughening,' Restel retorted. 'I've told you before. I am not having him mope about the place reading

81

those books. I wouldn't mind so much if it was the Bible but what he does read isn't healthy. He's becoming a real sissy.'

'Stuff and nonsense,' Cushla snapped. 'You should hear yourself.'

Mr Young came to see Restel one evening. Restel had been in the bath. Cushla made some tea and took it out onto the porch as Mr Young was in his working clobber.

'I'm filthy dirty, Mrs Bevan. Don't want to muck up your home. You work too hard keeping it clean,' and he gave her such a grin that Cushla felt a weakness in her knees. Mr Young was such a handsome brute. She'd always thought that. He was a true man and no mistake. As she fussed with the tea tray they talked about the weather, about the chances of there being a break from the heat. The local farmers were all expecting one.

'We've all got to pull together,' Mr Young told her. 'Bust our boilers until the rain comes.'

When Restel came out Cushla poured him a cuppa and went to go back inside. Mr Young stopped her, saying, 'I reckon you'll need to know this, Mrs Bevan. I came over to see you both,' and Cushla felt her face grow scarlet as he looked at her so directly, grinning his manly grin. Not daring to look at Restel, Cushla sat down again and stared at her lap. Restel didn't sit. She could feel his sight on her as Mr Young began to speak.

'I reckon I'll have to ask you to give up your free Sundays,' he said to Restel. 'I've no choice. I've blokes off crook, a couple have buggered off down to Canterbury and, Christ, I need all the help I can get.'

He shrugged, then glanced at Cushla and added, 'I'll pay you overtime of course, Restel. I'm a fair bloke and you're a bloody keen worker. I'm sorry about this, Mrs Bevan. I know you need the time to attend church with your husband but farming doesn't go with it at times like these. Not for me, at any rate. It's a bit of a bugger, I know.'

Restel's face had gone livid. Cushla started to say it was

all right, began to assure Mr Young but Restel cut her off.

'I won't have you blaspheming in front of my wife,' Restel said. 'We are Christian people. I put up with it in the day but not here, not in my own home!'

'Look, Bevan, get this straight, mate. This is my property, my house and I employ you. I respect your religion, too right, but I'm getting real riled at your Bible-slinging ways. You've upset quite a few of the blokes here, do you realize that?'

He was silent for a minute, seemed to become calm.

'So I reckon you either come down from now on Sundays or you're finished here. I mean it. It's up to you, mate. I'm an easy sort of bloke but there's a limit.'

He stepped down into the yard.

'Good night. Good night, Mrs Bevan. Ta for the cuppa. Lynette said to say thanks for the bottled pears you sent over. That was real beaut,' and he grinned at Cushla before turning away, moving off into the darkness. Cushla kept her eyes on him as his figure moulded into the night. He'd been wearing shorts and a black singlet, gumboots on his feet. She felt herself trembling a bit, though it was not just through worry. She had begun to develop feelings for Mr Young. His massive, muscular, hairy legs and that deep, manly chest. And his eyes, which seemed to stare down inside her whenever he was about. His eyes touched her soul and shook it up.

Restel went back indoors and she was alone there on the porch, her eyes still staring to where Mr Young had gone into the airless night. Cushla held onto the table as an overwhelming urge to walk out there into that darkness came over her. A need to call out Mr Young's name, go to him, be with him. Cushla drew up her hands, holding them over her face as if to block out all thought, but she could see his hands on her body and his lips pressed to her lips, suddenly ashamed and fearful and filled with panic, recalling the way he had looked at her at the get-together. The way his eyes had lingered on her breasts. She felt

83

worse when she realized that what he'd told Restel hadn't shook her a bit. That their not being able to go to church on Sundays, at this moment, meant nothing. All she wanted to do was go off in the dark with Mr Young and let him cover her body and penetrate it with the passion she knew was in him.

Restel began to talk to her about shifting again.

'I've been making some queries,' he told her quietly as they were getting ready for bed. 'There's plenty of work up north, in Auckland. I don't think we're cut out for farming. I feel the Lord would rather we move on. I've been praying about it and I know He will give me guidance.'

'What about another farm?' Cushla snapped. 'Some of the church people at Te Aroha, they have farms. One of them might need sharemilkers. Haven't you asked?'

Restel shook his head. 'It isn't that, Cushla. It's the life here. It's not healthy for the boys. I don't believe it's God's will for us to stay. We've been here long enough.'

'For goodness' sake!' Cushla almost shouted. 'Listen to what you're saying.'

They stood rigidly on either side of the bed, staring at each other. After a minute Restel turned away, picked up his Bible and sat on the bed with his back to her. He began to read.

'It isn't the boys,' Cushla said quietly. 'It's got nothing to do with them, has it? It's you. Finding fault with every job you've had. You should hear yourself! And you're taking it out on Billy. Where's the good, eh? Where's the good? It kills me when you belt him, it kills me!'

Restel placed his Bible face down on the bed, turning to look at her. His face was livid.

'You are my wife, Cushla, in subjection to me. Have you forgotten that? I run this family, I make decisions. That's the Christian way. Anything else is sin, do you hear me? I am not taking anything out on Billy. I'm making him into a man, like his brothers. I will not have a sissy under my roof.'

'You will turn him away,' Cushla said in a deep, dreadful whisper. 'You will destroy him.'

'Don't talk tripe,' Restel retorted. 'Sometimes I do wonder about you. I wonder if you aren't a bit touched, the way you talk.'

Cushla began to weep. She was still weeping when Restel got into bed, turned on his side. After a few minutes he began to whisper. He was praying to his God.

Some days Melvin drove over after Seddon got home from work, so they could go rabbit shooting together. Melvin took bottles of beer hidden in a rucksack and often when they returned after dark they'd be just a little bit shickered. Cushla noticed but kept her mouth shut, uncertain if Restel realized what they got up to. One evening they brought three dead rabbits back, one of them a pregnant female. Billy and Colin sat on the back steps to watch Melvin cleaning the rifles. When he'd finished he laid the rifles aside and picked up the pregnant rabbit. He was acting drunk, laughing and cracking jokes. Cushla watched from the kitchen window. Melvin pulled a knife from the pocket of his strides and slit the rabbit open along its underbelly. Three well-formed babies slid out and fell to the ground. Melvin picked one of them up, held it high and threw it at Billy. It hit Billy in the face and landed in his lap. Billy screamed in shock. Cushla went to rush out but was stopped by Seddon's shouting. Seddon almost leapt at Melvin, socking him in the jaw with a terrific wallop, yelling at him and calling him a bad bugger. Billy began to cry. Melvin fell on his bum and looked dazed for a few minutes. Seddon kicked him in the leg and told him to push off out of it, Melvin struggling to his feet and fetching the rifles, standing beside the open door of his car for a long time with a queer, savage look across his face. His sight rested first on Billy, then Seddon.

'You wait, you bastard,' he said. 'You just wait.'

As he roared off down the road in his car he honked the horn several times. Each of them heard his laughter. It remained in the cool night air after he'd gone, a harsh and bitter sound. As far as Cushla knew he didn't come to the house again after that. She made Seddon bury two of the dead rabbits and the babies, cooked the third one the following day in a stew. Neither Billy nor Seddon would touch it. Seddon refused even to sit down at the table and sulked in his room, after giving her a glaring look of disgust.

One Saturday a few weeks later, Colin got crook. He'd been in the sun for too long and because of his ginger colouring blisters had come out on his shoulders and across the top of his chest. He threw up all over the kitchen floor. Cushla was pretty shook. Colin, although always quiet, was stronger than Seddon. She tucked him into bed after washing the blisters as gently as she could and mopping up the sick. It wasn't serious enough to call in a doctor yet it added to her low spirits of the last few days.

Seddon had two crates of beer hidden down at the milking sheds. Melvin had got the beer for him some time back. Since the get-together gave him a taste for it, Seddon had been spending time down at the shed drinking beer with the men whenever his dad wasn't about. The other older sharemilkers reckoned it was a bit of a dag, knew it couldn't do any real harm. They were all pretty fed up with Seddon's dad anyway, going on about salvation to them whenever he got the chance. There was no reason why Bevan's oldest boy shouldn't have a go at the booze, he seemed to enjoy it. Nothing was ever said to Restel.

Seddon had removed a dozen full bottles from the sheds, tied string to the necks and hidden them in the cool stream which ran through the bush behind the house, securing the string to stakes in the bank. He'd been spending a lot of time down there alone since he'd rowed with Melvin. The day after Colin got crook from the sun Seddon took Billy with him down to the stream while Restel was somewhere off on the farm, working for the first time in his life on a Sunday. Cushla had decided to have a lie down. Colin was fast asleep.

Far off along the side of a hill Restel was clearing scrub with some of the other sharemilkers. The men there had beer too, guzzling it back beneath the scorching sun. All sweated buckets, all swore as the gorse ripped their flesh, all shared jokes and swapped tall tales of past glory. All except Restel, who worked alone, separated from the men he could not call his mates. Occasionally he sipped from a bottle of water beside him, wiping his brow with a sweat-darkened hanky and staring at the sky. Despite the company of these men he'd begun to pity and pray for, he had for a time felt at one with his Lord, here on this rich, fertile land. Yet the shadows of dissension and sin were reaching out even here, to where he'd believed they would be closer to heaven. Perhaps it was time they did shift. Go north to seek out that place where the foundations of their lives could be built upon, in the glory of His name.

Colin was lying in bed, covered only by a sheet, the windows of his room wide open and the fly screen preventing any insects from entering. Through the window he had seen Seddon and Billy going off across the back paddock towards the bush. Seddon had his arm round Billy's shoulders. The ground beneath their feet shimmered in the heat, as if they were walking on water.

After a while, lying there so still, the sound of cicadas caused Colin's drowsiness to return. His eyes slowly closed, he sighed then he slept. He remembered what he had viewed later as if it had been part of his dreaming.

Cushla nodded off for an hour lying on top of the bed. She woke with a terrific thirst, went out to the kitchen for a drink, plugging in the jug to boil water for a cuppa. Then she saw the brown-paper bag on the sideboard without at first registering what it held, picking it up and realizing it was Restel's sandwiches, his lunch. She stood there undecided for a minute, knowing that where Restel was working was too far for her to go herself, recalling that Mr Young would be down at the milking sheds whitewashing the walls, as Restel had said he would be. She could take the sandwiches down there with a fresh bottle of water and someone could drive out to Restel on the tractor. He'd need his lunch, no mistake; he could not get back for it himself.

Cushla unplugged the jug, put on her gumboots and let herself out the back door, closing it quietly. She had peeped in on Colin. He was sleeping, his face pale and his mouth wide open. She reckoned he'd be in bed for a few days yet. There was no sign of Seddon or Billy about the place. She filled a milk bottle from the outside tap where the water was cooler, pulled up from below ground. She stood there for a long time, staring out across the land, above which rain clouds were now forming, unsure now if she could face Mr Young. She would be alone with him, down there at the sheds. Should he make any move towards her she would not be able to turn away. Cushla had no idea if he felt the same way about her as she felt about him. She'd not had much experience with men, did not understand them. She often wondered why she had married at all. It had simply been expected of her. Restel had for a time opened some feelings inside her she'd never been aware of, only to have those feelings and desires become a deep frustration within her as the years passed by. Mr Young had touched a nerve and it scared her. Cushla shivered. She had a duty to Restel. There was no hurry. She had no excuse not to go. If she took the long way through the bush it'd help her to calm down, to feel a little cooler, the sun now so high and the heat intense. She couldn't remember when rain had last fallen, but the weather was changing. The heat wouldn't stay forever.

She was only halfway across the paddock when she felt a queer chill skitter down her back, though there was no reason for it. She stopped, looked about her but no one was in sight. Cushla walked slowly, thoughts of Mr Young still filling her head. She knew she was delaying the moment when she'd set eyes on him. A tension gathered inside her, an excited longing she reckoned was wrong. Yet it was there, and was so real. Nothing could come of her feelings for him, she knew that. At least no one else could know of her thoughts.

Cushla followed the bush track, so the gorse and the huge ferns wouldn't catch at her. She came to the place where Seddon and Billy were by the stream suddenly, just as she saw Mr Young through the trees, walking from the direction of the sheds. He saw her at the same time. He waved and grinned and quickened his pace towards her as Cushla looked back to Seddon and Billy, who hadn't seen her at all.

Cushla's hands fluttered up to her mouth and she dropped the sandwiches and the water bottle. Her hands clawed across her mouth as she stared at what her boys were doing, there on the earth beside the gurgling water.

Empty beer bottles lay strewn across the scrub-cleared ground. There must have been at least a dozen lying there. Seddon stood holding a bottle against his chest, leaning against a tree, his head pulled back, face to the sky. His eyes were shut. Neither of the boys was wearing clothes, though Billy still wore underpants which looked like they'd been rubbed in the dirt. Billy was kneeling down in front of Seddon. His arms were clasped tightly round Seddon's legs. Seddon's erect penis was in Billy's mouth.

Cushla cried out, just as Mr Young entered the clearing from the other side, and it was he who Seddon saw first, opening his eyes, not Cushla, yet she reckoned he was aware of her there at the same moment. In one violent movement Seddon pushed Billy away from him, turned and ran, the bottle of beer flying from his hands to fall and smash on a rock beside the water, its froth jetting out over Billy who'd fallen to his side. Seddon ran naked across the shallow stream, stumbling then falling, scrambling to his feet and fleeing as Billy sat up staring over at his mum, grinning from ear to ear. Billy tried to stand up, then he too stumbled. He began to giggle helplessly, attempting to find his shorts and shirt from amongst Seddon's discarded clothing. Cushla was unable to move, knowing that Mr Young had also seen her boys there beside the water. Mr Young did not utter a sound. After one horrified glance at Cushla he turned and retraced his steps. With long, determined strides he hurried back out of the bush and down the slope towards the milking sheds, not stopping until he was out of sight. Cushla stood with her hands clasped over her mouth staring at Billy, who was so obviously drunk. He had stopped giggling but the laughter's obscene echo still tore through Cushla's skull.

She ran to him then, forgetting all else, grabbing hold so roughly his head twisted as he tried to pull away from her with a cry of pain. They struggled there silently while she got him dressed, leaving Seddon's clothes where they lay. Cushla pulled Billy by the arm back along the bush track, Billy falling over every few yards, across the paddock and into the house. She shut Billy into his room, slamming his door, ignoring Colin.

'Mum, Mum, what's happening?' he was calling out.

Cushla went back outside, across the paddock again,

almost running, to fetch the sandwiches and water. Peering down the track without seeing a sign of Seddon, standing there so long in silence it made her think there was no one else alive, no one for her to turn to, as she would not, could not tell Restel of what she had seen. Shaking like a leaf, recalling the look on Mr Young's face, she had no idea whether he would say a word. What could he say, even to Restel? How could she, whose boys they were, explain what her and Mr Young had witnessed?

Seddon still hadn't appeared when Restel came back after dark. Cushla let him think the boys were in bed, as it was late. Billy she'd bathed and put into his pyjamas. He'd been so drunk he'd hardly been able to stand up. Now he slept deeply and she knew he would not wake until the morning. She'd told Colin nothing. Yet in his eyes he'd known something was up.

Restel was having a soak in the bath when Seddon finally came in through the back door. He looked pale and dishevelled. He would not look Cushla in the eye. He trembled. She put his tea on the table, silently watched him trying to eat before he suddenly shot up from his chair and rushed off to his room after one long dreadful look at her face. Neither of them spoke a word to one another. The pain that gave Cushla made her weep when he'd left the kitchen. She hadn't known what on earth to say to him.

Restel had been in bed for hours when she went through to their room. He had given her a telling-off once he'd finished his bath, having noticed his sandwiches sitting on the table where Cushla had left them. He had a go at her because she hadn't got one of the boys to take them to him, when he was working so hard to keep a roof over their heads.

He was snoring as she closed the door of the bedroom behind her. From the bush out the back moreporks were calling. Just before dawn, as Cushla lay there still wide-awake, rain finally began to fall, and thunder sounded, from the sky.

In the following weeks came what Cushla reckoned was a fluke of timing, allowing her to suppress, at least for a while, full memory of that afternoon. Restel told Mr Young he was not able to work again on Sundays. His faith in his Lord Jesus Christ would not allow it. He was consequently told a while after that his sharemilking days, at least here on this farm, were over. They were given no more than a week's notice to clear out of the house. Cushla's fear changed to panic, then relief, before a numbing exhaustion took over.

'He used the Saviour's name as a curse,' Restel told her. 'I was ashamed I've worked for such a man. He told me that people like us had no place here,' then he stared and stared at her for so long and so strangely she shuddered and looked away from his gaze in confusion.

'We'll pack up and go to Auckland,' Restel continued. 'There's work up there. I've still got some of the money Bulla loaned us. It'll be enough. I'm writing to Bulla, I'll have to tell her everything,' and he still stared at Cushla intently for such a long time that she rushed from the room, unable to bear his eyes on her for another minute. She could not believe that Mr Young could've said anything to Restel about Seddon and Billy. No, it wasn't credible, not at all. Restel would have blown his top, shouted at her, accused her. Wouldn't he? He wouldn't be speaking as calmly as he was.

They were in the midst of packing when Seddon came to her and told her he wanted to stay put. His boss at the garage in Morrinsville didn't reckon he should leave, had sent a letter which Seddon handed to her, a friendly letter full of praise for his work, offering to board Seddon until the first part of his apprenticeship was completed. He was a good, keen lad, the letter read. They would look after him like he was their own, the boss and his wife. There was no question in Cushla's mind, when she'd read the letter.

'It'd be better, Mum,' Seddon said, white-faced. 'It'll be all right, no mistake. It'd be better,' and he hung his head and went out back to where clouds now scudded across the sky, to where he could not see her eyes.

Restel hadn't argued or objected, despite Seddon being pretty young to be off on his own. He'd agreed almost straight off, which shook Cushla to the core as Seddon's boss was not a Christian man. That should have told Cushla a lot about Restel's recent staring at her, the reasons for it, but everything was happening too fast, her mind was so confused. She'd almost decided that Restel knew nothing of what had gone on, even less able to mention it now than at the time. She tried to pretend it hadn't happened at all.

She and Restel drove over to Morrinsville one night in the Chrysler, without Seddon, had tea with the garage boss and his wife, saw where Seddon would live and agreed to the arrangements, hardly even discussing them on the way home. Chugging along the dark country road, they sat far apart on the front seat.

The week they had left to pack was a busy, strained, silent time. Colin was the only one who seemed cheery. Cushla kept looking for Mr Young when she was out the back hanging up the washing, wanting to see him yet terrified of an encounter. He'd called Restel down to his office at the sheds when he'd given notice, hadn't come near the house since then. Not seeing him created a frightened anger inside Cushla which she tried her darnedest to control. She found herself belting Colin one morning, hitting him again and again across his legs for no more reason than he'd broken two of her good plates. She couldn't stand Billy near her. She tried not to think about anything but Billy was there, all the time, staring at her with a need for comfort but she shied away. Restel noticed but said nothing at all. Seddon kept away and was off on the farm whenever he could escape.

They packed everything into the trailer and the car. Cleaned the house, tidied the yards front and back. Restel stayed home and helped her, refusing to go down to the sheds at all. Cushla stacked all the preserves she'd bottled on the table, for Lynette, with a note. The rain continued to fall, on and off, the whole week. Low cloud hung over the paddocks and over the bush. Before the Saturday when they were expected to leave, Seddon's boss drove over from Morrinsville to collect him. Cushla had packed his things into two suitcases.

Their goodbyes were hurried, and painful. They had been living under a tension almost too sharp to bear. The atmosphere during those days drained each of them. They were like blinded strangers, waiting for some kind of redemption.

Thunder boomed in the distance, as they left the farm. Driving off along the deserted road before dusk fell on the Saturday night, they headed north. Neither Mr Young nor Lynette had come over to say hooray. Restel had booked them into a motel somewhere up in Auckland, by writing to the place urgently at the beginning of the week and getting a prompt reply. The trip would not be a long one. In the silence in the car Cushla and Restel exchanged a cautious look.

Then he told her, 'It'll be all right up north. You'll see. Auckland's a big place. Good weather too. It'll be cleaner. I'll find work, with our Lord's help,' falling silent as more thunder sounded. It was the most he had said to her all week, Cushla reckoned, peering forward through the windscreen. On the road ahead possums' eyes were reflecting from the glow of the headlamps. The rain had eased off, for the time being. But not too far north as they drove into the dark beyond, a violent storm was gathering its forces together, across the land.

Part Three

People shouldn't make ripples
Ripples can form
into waves and
no one likes being
drowned.

                                    Billy Bevan

City of Sparkling Water

They were living in a pokey flat at Mount Albert, a suburb of Auckland city, when Bulla suddenly died. The news shook Restel far more than it did Cushla. Bulla had been killed as she was stepping into her bath. She had slipped, grabbed hold of the electric heater on the shelf by mistake. The heater had been switched on. There was an uncertainty whether Bulla had drowned or been electrocuted, as the heater fell into the water with her and she'd cracked her head open. But she'd died, and Restel was preparing to go down on the train for the funeral, leaving Cushla with Colin and Billy. There were Bulla's affairs to sort out and the will to be read. The funeral, apparently, was to be arranged by the church-goers she'd worshipped with on Sundays.

Until then, the shift to Auckland had proved to be plain sailing, despite Seddon not being with them. Or because of it, Cushla reckoned at odd moments when she remembered things and was feeling low. Billy had got into the local grammar school which was a pretty flash place; he had to sit a test to get in. He was deliriously happy, had recently brought home the school magazine in which two of his poems had been published. Colin had begun work as an apprentice carpenter in a factory at nearby Mount Roskill. Having two of her boys in trades made Cushla real proud. Restel was an office clerk in town, quite a well-paid job with prospects but they were still short and Cushla was forced to watch the pennies and scrimp quite a bit. Billy's uniform and school books had set them back. Now there was the burden of money worries over Restel's trip down to Wellington on the train. He'd got unpaid time off work. He was so determined to go Cushla hadn't the heart to point out that the money spent would be cutting into even more of Bulla's loan. They'd have nothing to fall back on should any of them get crook.

Cushla had received a letter from Bulla before she'd been killed, which she hadn't shown Restel nor mentioned, even after the news had come through that Bulla was dead. The letter had been addressed personally to Cushla. Bulla's words had really got Cushla's ire up. She'd been so wild the news of Bulla's tragedy hardly caused more than a ripple of shock, which later brought a dreadful guilt to her heart.

Dear Cushla, the letter read:

> I told Restel I would be writing to you so I'm not going behind his back. As he is my younger brother I have always watched over his well-being and I feel I ought to point out the error of your ways, which is worrying Restel sick. He has written to me as his sister and as a fellow-Christian and I must say I am shocked and worried at your lack of gumption in dealing with Restel's boys. Their true salvation will never come about if you continue to let them get away with the sinning Restel has written to me about, for which he holds you responsible. I need not point out that you yourself took the Lord to be your guide after you married my brother. You must find it in your heart to make certain the flesh of my brother's loins will not fall by the wayside and perish, through filth. Do pray for guidance, sister dear, and watch your health, especially your bowels.
> Your loving sister in law in Christ,
> Bulla.

Cushla had gone beetroot by the time she'd read the

letter a couple of times. At first she planned to have it out with Restel, find out what he'd been writing to his sister, then decided she would write back and tear a strip off Bulla. In the end she did neither, put the letter in the bottom drawer of her dresser and forced the matter out of her mind, until the news of Bulla's death dragged it up again.

Billy had asked Cushla if he could have the loan of one of her brassieres, for a skit he was to act in at the grammar school concert. The concert was to be held at the Auckland Town Hall. Billy had joined the school drama club. He needed the brassiere for his role as an ugly sister in a skit on Cinderella.

'They asked us to ask our mums,' Billy told her. 'Some of the others have already got their costumes. I can fill the brassiere with cotton-wool, it'd look real neat!' and he'd given her a huge grin. Cushla was so wild at him she felt like flouncing off to see Billy's headmaster and having a go. When she mentioned it to Restel he grew very pale and cut her off from saying anything more, making her wish she'd kept her mouth shut. Later that night in the bathroom with the door locked Restel whipped Billy's legs with a length of rubber hose he'd taken to using, without saying a word to Billy about what he'd done to deserve it – though Billy was now given beatings without there having to be much of a reason. Cushla was getting sick to death of it. She was so angry at Restel using the piece of rubber hose she took it and threw it in the bin when Restel was out. Nothing more was said about the concert. In the end Cushla allowed Billy to go, Restel washing his hands of the matter. Billy told her his friend would help with the costume. He was also singing in a small choir on the night, his form master had written a letter, requesting permission. Neither Cushla nor Restel had gone to the concert as a kind of extra punishment. And because it took place on the evening of the day they received the cable about Bulla. Billy had sulked about their not going for days after. Cushla overheard him telling Colin all about it. There was now in Billy's voice something she had not sensed nor heard before, something not quite right in the way he spoke. She'd noticed it recently in his gestures too, the way his hands fluttered about as he spoke, yet it was his telling Colin what he had worn in the Cinderella skit which made Cushla feel a sharp pain in her heart. Colin had scoffed and said he thought it all a real load of claptrap, dressing up like a girl in front of all those people. Billy was getting to be a real little pansy. Cushla had almost shouted at Colin, she was so wild over that. Yet both Colin and Seddon had been growing up to be proper little blokes, the way all New Zealand boys did. Billy, Billy with his shining, grinning face almost too pretty for a boy, Billy with his laughter and his funny little ways, was different. She'd always known that he was special, saved by medical marvel. Cushla loved Billy desperately. She felt so ill and hot with temper whenever Restel belted him now as he never belted Seddon or Colin. Yet there was growing a fear, a dread of what that specialness, this difference of Billy's could be. It'd been Restel who thought a boys' school would be good for him, might toughen Billy up a bit, help him find a trade he could enter once he'd finished his learning, a trade both Cushla and Restel could be proud of his getting into. Yet this school didn't seem to have any interest in encouraging normal, manly interests at all. Billy's interest in books, and poetry, and now the drama club which he talked about all the time, filled his waking hours. It made his difference more marked. That deepened Cushla's dread, despite the love in her heart. With the love still there she tried to push everything else aside. She tried not to fret over things about Billy she couldn't fully grasp.

After they'd reached Auckland, stayed for weeks at the

motel, found the flat at Mount Albert which proved to be a real flash, moneyed area, life had certainly gone along a lot more smoothly. Both Cushla and Restel got on a bit better. They'd toured the sights round Auckland at weekends in the Chrysler with the boys, driving over to the North Shore for picnics on Takapuna beach which they'd taken a liking to, driving round the waterfront beside the Waitemata, Auckland's harbour, which sparkled and looked so pretty beneath the brilliant sun. Cushla hadn't suffered any chest problems at all since the shift, and Restel had found his job in town almost straight away. He was already talking about their possibly renting a house somewhere further out. The flat lay at the end of a long narrow alley lined with flowering bush and kowhai trees, one flat in a row of five with car ports. There was little privacy. None of the neighbours seemed all that friendly, were mostly young couples starting out. The lack of room meant that should Seddon come up from Morrinsville there'd be nowhere for him to doss down. A rented house was the only answer. Restel had been making a few enquiries when Bulla died. Now he was going off down there for a few weeks leaving Cushla to run things, with little money.

She knew that they were both ignoring the recent past, pretending to themselves on the surface that they were starting out fresh, that what had been going on was dead and buried. Both of them would stare at each other at odd moments, unwilling and unable to discuss or rake up anything, living under the impression that silence was a good thing. Laughter between them was a bit forced, unnatural. And into that laughter was seeping a sort of panic.

Cushla went to see Restel off at the railway station in Auckland. Restel wore a black arm-band Cushla had stitched to his overcoat. He pecked her on the cheek at the barrier as he said hooray. Hardly had he walked away from her down the platform when Cushla was off like a shot to ring up from the City PO about a temporary job she'd seen advertised in the newspaper. A typing job at Mount Albert in a solicitor's office for three weeks, just down the road from the flat. It'd suit her right to the ground, bring in some extra money while Restel was away. She didn't have to tell him about it. She had wasted her work experience since she married him. Before the marriage she'd held a heck of a good job at Government House in Wellington, had kept her reference, an excellent one she was proud of. Restel still didn't want her working, had forced her to give up that other job long ago when they'd got engaged. This temporary job was only to tide her and the boys over. The idea excited Cushla. That evening, with her appointment settled for the following afternoon, she sat and helped Billy with his algebra homework, which he hated. She let both of them stay up late. She hugged her boys, a bit choked up, before they went to bed, not telling them about the typing job in case she didn't get it. Instead, she said to Billy in a tremulous voice, 'I feel bad that we didn't come to your concert. Your dad wouldn't let me come, reckoned your dressing up was sinful. Perhaps next year, eh? I'll come and I won't tell Dad,' ducking her head and grinning at him as he grinned back and told her that it was all right, he didn't really mind.

Cushla sat in the tiny front room and hummed hymns to herself for the rest of the evening, thinking about what she could wear for the interview tomorrow, pleased that she could walk to the solicitor's office down at the shops, it was so handy, even thinking about taking the boys on a spree into town with the extra money, perhaps to the pictures at one of the flash Auckland theatres she'd seen along Queen Street. Before long it was midnight and she reckoned she'd better get off to bed, there was not much of the night left. She'd need her beauty sleep, for the big event the next day.

Restel sat beside the window, staring out at the land as the train travelled south, his heart heavy and his face grey with tiredness and worry. He was almost pleased to be getting away, although the shock of Bulla's dreadful death had hit him for a six. He had loved Bulla deeply as she had cared so much for him in the past, when they were young. An awful sense of aloneness washed over him and he choked from the memories, turning his head at an even sharper angle away from the other travellers in the carriage, in case they should witness his weakness. A lady opposite had been staring at his black arm-band the whole time since they'd left the station, seemed keen to catch his eye and speak, as New Zealanders did so readily to each other, with such openness.

The recent past, Cushla's secretive behaviour, his inability to find an employer who respected his commitment to Christ; all this made him fear for the future, being cast aside because his family, he believed, might be stepping onto a different path. He had disciplined Billy in the hope that it would make changes. Billy was so unlike his brothers. Restel believed that in the name of Christ he had to remove that impudence and the sissiness before it took hold and began to destroy his youngest son.

Cushla genuinely believed that Billy had been saved for some special reason in life, something in the future. Perhaps that was why she'd not told Restel about the goings on at the farm between Seddon and Billy.

He knew all about it. Mr Young had told him. He'd tried to deny it. Done nothing about it for he felt in his heart that such disgusting filth could not possibly be true. That it was a wicked lie attacking his faith. Cushla's belief in Billy's specialness was so strong. Yet why had he not said a word either, to Cushla, with whom he shared the

105

love of Christ? Was what had happened there between the boys, if even a scrap of it was true, too damning, too filthy and sickening to voice?

Thoughts crowded together in Restel's mind as the train gathered speed. Without removing his gaze from the land beyond the glass he reached into the small suitcase on his lap, brought out his Bible, opening it at random, and lowered his gaze to its words of comfort and hope. He did not allow his sight to rise up and meet that of the nosey parker opposite, who sat there so still, watching him with a stare of sympathy and compassion. Restel knew his expression would be revealing his anguish. He was that kind of man, had always been so. Fearing weakness. He knew quite simply that should he look up and meet those eyes he would begin to weep.

Cushla was so excited when she left the solicitors' office after her interview she went straight into the butchers' and bought three T-bone steaks, thrusting the shock of the price back into her head as far as it would go, cheerfully chatting with the butcher who reminded her of Mr Young, a real handsome brute who winked at her as she left and stared at her legs when she glanced over her shoulder at him through the window outside. She had almost told him about being offered the job but feared he might think she was being forward, or having a flirt. With the sudden freedom she felt, a glow of pleasure inside her, she sauntered back up to the flat, enjoying the late sunshine and the posh homes she stared into, thinking of Restel with only a tiny bit of sadness at his loss. Knowing that Bulla had enjoyed a pretty good life, hadn't lingered with some wasteful disease like TB or being senile. Cushla suddenly felt an overwhelming kindness towards Bulla, despite that awful letter she'd sent before death had taken her.

*

Billy wrote poetry in the evenings after they'd had tea, and Cushla thought of buying him a cheap second-hand typewriter which he'd be sure to find handy. She decided to have a look for one on the quiet. Perhaps he would get famous one day, become a poet and prove her belief that he was special. Was this why he'd been saved, to be a poet? She could not imagine it to be any more than a hobby for anyone, something like that. It couldn't ever be a real job of work like the trades Seddon and Colin were getting into. She'd no idea what Restel would make of Billy's developing arty-farty ways, but for the time being that didn't matter.

Billy had brought a friend home from school one afternoon. He insisted on Cushla doing tea and cakes and providing serviettes and sitting down properly in their tiny front room. His friend acted very posh and kept staring at Cushla as if he couldn't believe she was Billy's mum, despite her having put on her best frock and scrubbed her face until it shone. He and Billy talked in rapid, high voices about poets and writers. Billy skited about the New Zealand poet James K. Baxter who'd taught Billy for a little while in the primers. Cushla sat there trying to act interested but half the things they discussed she'd never heard of. She felt quite shook at how Billy spoke with his friend from Nottingham in the Old Country, who'd only been in New Zealand a year and talked as if he had twenty plums in his mouth. He was very polite, and his name was Martin Royston-Carte. Billy had been going frequently to his house, a huge place on the slopes of the Mount above the school, where he lived with his mum and dad and a woman who'd been his nanny. Cushla found Martin to be a bit of a drip, but so well mannered. He was startlingly pale. Colin made her face go scarlet when he came in from work. Martin was just leaving, saying such nice things to her too. Colin burst out laughing when he heard Martin's voice and stared at the boy with a real scoffing expression. After he'd gone

Colin said what a heck of a sissy the boy was, just the sort of mate Billy would have at that school where no girls were. It really got Cushla's ire up, Colin's sneering. She decided she would try acting a bit more posh in future, in front of Martin Royston-Carte. For Billy's sake, and through her desperate need to love him.

Cushla's aloneness disturbed her a bit after Restel had been away almost a week. The feeling of freedom became stronger. Her job was only for a few hours in the morning, now she'd begun, although the money was good, and she'd seen an old but working typewriter for Billy down at the shops. She had been saving and already had nearly enough money for a day out in town for the three of them, which might stop Colin picking on Billy such a lot now Seddon wasn't there. Colin was being a real little wretch to Billy. The work at the solicitor's was so easy she found herself working out a better filing system and asking for extra jobs while she was there. She knew the partners were very pleased with her.

On the Friday, just before she was about to tidy up her desk and go home, her boss came out of his office and handed her an envelope, inside which was not only a full week's pay but a bonus. It shook her so much she went quite scarlet and felt such a fool trying to say thanks, stuttering, becoming flustered when her mouth went dry and her speech clicked loudly. Not that he seemed to notice, at least he didn't show it. Both partners were such well-spoken blokes, a bit hoity-toity but people like that always were. They were genuine, she reckoned. They'd asked her if she would like to work for them full-time at the end of the three weeks, named a salary which shook Cushla to the core as it was far more money than Restel got. She reckoned she'd better talk it over with him when he got back from Wellington, left in a welter of confusion and excitement, and went to buy the typewriter for Billy and a newspaper to see if there was a picture on in town they could go and see the next day.

She arranged for the typewriter, wrapped in brown paper with Billy's name on it, to be taken up the road to the flat and left at the back door, where he'd find it when he came home from school. He had a back-door key. It excited her to think of him finding it.

Cushla decided to go the whole hog and get her hair done, something else she hadn't been allowed to do since her marriage. She rang up a hairdresser's in Avondale from a public box, found they could fit her in just after lunch, and walked down to the bus stop at the bottom of the hill. She'd have some lunch in Avondale, a pie and a milkshake somewhere, and look at the shops, perhaps find a little something for Colin. Cushla had not felt so good for ages. She waited at the bus stop wanting to sing.

Restel and Cushla had started to go to a church in town, just off the Karangahape Road. They'd gone most Sundays although the boys had not attended any Bible classes and Restel hadn't yet gone to prayer meetings in the week, telling her that it would take a while for them to get settled. The Lord wouldn't mind; it was only for a while that they wouldn't be going to worship as much as they should. Cushla welcomed the break. She enjoyed the sense of freedom their not going every five minutes gave her. While Restel was away it would be too difficult to get into town on a Sunday morning as the bus service wasn't too good, so none of them would be going to church at all. The Chrysler was parked in the provided car port but, of course, Cushla couldn't drive. She had no idea how Restel would react, when he did get home, to her not making any effort. Yet as far as Cushla was concerned being a Christian was also acting with goodness and kindness and finding understanding. Now things were going so well she could be all those things, with the boys she loved so much. Besides, going to church without fail and all that self-denial business so you could receive your reward in heaven didn't do anyone a scrap of good at all, if you didn't enjoy yourself before you kicked the bucket.

On the way back from the hairdresser's, her newly permed and styled hair tied down with a flash chiffon scarf she had splashed out on, she heard a voice call out, 'Yoo hoo Mrs Bevan, yoo hoo!' And when she looked it was a woman she thought she knew but couldn't place, crossing the road as Cushla stepped off the bus holding the scarf in place from the wind and carrying a box of assorted chisels she'd brought as a present for Colin. Her hair had been back-combed so much it felt like it was standing up a mile. Cushla felt her face go pink when she realized who the woman was, although she still couldn't for the life of her remember the woman's name. That must have showed in her face as the woman said, catching up with her, 'I'm Phoebe Croft, don't you remember me, Cushla? From church?'

Cushla managed a laugh, saying, 'Oh, of course, how are you, Mrs Croft?'

'Call me Phoebe, dear sister, please do! And I'm not married, at least not yet!' and she tittered so loudly Cushla glanced round to see if the awful sound had attracted any attention. The woman was staring like a hawk at Cushla's hairdo.

'You look quite different, Cushla, I hardly recognized you! Are you off out somewhere then while hubby's away? We haven't seen you at worship lately, you have been missed, sister! We're having a working bee soon, next Friday. I'm certain you'll want to come, it's for the starving kiddies overseas. I could arrange to have you collected in the car if you like. Mrs Heckley's hubby is

110

collecting ladies from all over the place. I'm organizing that! One more won't make any difference!' and she continued to talk and titter all the way up the avenue until they reached the alley and Cushla had no alternative but to invite the dreadful woman in for a cup of tea. She'd been asking non-stop questions about the boys. Cushla told her about Colin learning to be a carpenter and Seddon's apprenticeship down in Morrinsville and Billy doing so well at the grammar school.

'I say, Billy must be a brainy boy to get in there,' Phoebe Croft said. 'He's your baby, isn't he, Cushla? I remember him now, such a beaudy-looking young bloke, such big blue eyes!'

When she spoke she put her face up real close and sprayed Cushla with saliva. Her breath ponged.

'He'll be doing his swotting,' Cushla told the woman as they reached the end of the alley. 'He has a lot of learning to do, every afternoon,' hoping the woman might get the hint. She suddenly decided that it was an awful idea, inviting this nosey parker in. She'd never get rid of her, going on and on like that as if she'd known Cushla for years.

'Your hair looks interesting, sister,' Phoebe Croft said as Cushla was unlocking the front door. Cushla nearly dropped her key and her packages she felt so nervous.

There was music coming from the front room as they stepped into the tiny hall. It was dance music, something old-fashioned. Cushla could hear laughter. She wasn't certain that Colin would be home yet as it was too early. She'd thought Billy would be hard at it with his home-work. The woman stepped through the door in front of her with her neck craning, her tiny dark eyes darting about all over the place. Then she looked into the front room and stopped moving. Cushla almost had to push past her, the woman was standing right in the doorway.

111

At first Cushla thought the figure dancing by itself in the centre of the room was a very short woman with huge breasts. The figure was wearing a floor-length ball-gown, a fox fur draped about the shoulders and coloured feathers in her hair, swaying to and fro to the music and singing in a high-pitched somehow false voice. When the figure fully turned round revealing a face plastered with make-up, bright red lips and long eyelashes, Cushla saw that it was Billy. Not far from him, leaning against the settee beside a record player placed on a table, holding a lighted cigarette up high and the stance like a woman's with the wrist bent back and the other hand on his hip, stood Martin Royston-Carte. They had the blinds pulled down and the music so loud it was a full minute before either of them noticed Cushla and Phoebe Croft there. It was when the woman began to make dreadful tittering sounds and cried out, 'Oh, my giddy aunt!' that they were noticed. It all happened so quickly. Billy simply stood there staring with his mouth open and Martin began to giggle and look Phoebe Croft up and down. She was such a sight there, with her mouth wide open, so dowdy and plain. Each of them froze for what seemed to be a long time, until Cushla, unable to bear the tension, said in as posh a voice as she could muster, 'Oh, there you are, Billy. This is Mrs Croft from church. She's ever so keen to hear all about you!'

Something Unsettling in their Gaze

They walked arm in arm from the bus stop, Cushla, Colin and Billy, down the slope of Queen Street towards the ferry building along the quay. There was a stiff breeze and cloud scattered across the sky and the smell of the sea was strong. As it was Saturday the shops were shut but they sauntered along peering in all the windows. Billy insisted they cross over and look in Whitcombe and Tombe's window which had a display of poetry books by James K. Baxter and Denis Glover and photographs of other poets and writers Billy worshipped. He knew so many things about people that Cushla had never heard of. She wondered where his braininess had come from.

A couple of nights ago she'd dreamed that Billy was not their son, that she'd given birth to a different Billy who'd died and they'd adopted a little boy with the same name. The dream had shook her so much she hadn't slept a wink all the rest of the night. The sheets, when she'd woken with an awful cry, had been drenched with perspiration.

Billy and Colin had not been keen on an outing. They'd had a moan about it as both of them said they had other things to do. Cushla was taking them on the ferry across to Devonport to look at the shops there and have a picnic on the beach. She'd made sandwiches and cooked some whitebait fritters and savaloys, up at five that morning to get it all ready on her own. She had bottles of fizz for each of them and packed the lot into her huge shopping bag which Colin was lugging. She'd had to turf both of them out of bed by eight o'clock so they could get going. They'd grizzled a bit but cheered up when she gave them some pocket money, despite Colin not needing any now he worked. She'd bought herself a brand new frock and a gorgeous sun hat made from flax. New shorts, bright colourful shirts and plastic sandals for the boys. She felt quite proud marching down Queen Street her boys on either side with their arms through hers. They'd cheered up a bit more having reached town and she felt excited, with money in her purse and her new hairdo which still looked all right. She'd even added a touch of colour to her lips. She kept a lipstick hidden in her dresser but wouldn't dare use it once Restel got back. She was making the best of it, she reckoned, while he was away.

It had come over a little cloudy by the time they'd walked to the bottom of Queen Street and crossed over to the ferry building. Billy had stopped at each of the theatres along the way, staring at the photos outside. She hoped he'd be excited when they came back over the harbour as she planned for them to go to a two o'clock picture show. *South Pacific* was on at the Plaza. She'd heard a great deal about the film, it'd been on for ages, the longest run of any picture show in Auckland, according to one of the typists at the solicitor's. The girl had been to see the film with her young bloke and had whetted Cushla's appetite.

Cushla felt so good keeping the extra shout a secret, held her boys' arms tightly, grinning all the way. They went into the ferry building and had a look round before buying some apples to eat, from the kiosk, and tickets for the trip across the harbour; the boat was waiting to leave the wharf in ten minutes. When they walked through the barrier and clambered up the wooden plank onto the ferry, Cushla said she'd sit inside as it was a bit blowy.

'You can have a look round if you like,' she told Colin, settling herself down near a window so she could admire the view. 'The driver won't mind. You can see the engine and the boilers!' Perhaps she'd have a natter with the two Maori ladies who gave her such huge, friendly grins and made room so she could sit beside them.

One of the ladies said, 'Looks like it could bloody piss down, eh,' as Cushla put her bag beside her. She felt a bit put out by the words but reckoned the lady was just being friendly. Both of them started to fire questions at her about the boys, straight off, after Colin and Billy shot off upstairs to watch the ferry leaving the wharf. In no time at all Cushla was chatting away nineteen to the dozen. Enjoying a good laugh. The Maori ladies told her all about Auckland, having found out Cushla had shifted here from the south. One of them said she'd seen *South Pacific* four times and wept quite a bit and was certain Cushla would, and knew some of the songs off by heart. She sang one to Cushla in a most beautiful voice.

The ferry was soon chugging across the water. The harbour was named the Waitemata, which in English meant 'sparkling waters', the Maori ladies said. Most days the harbour did sparkle, stretching out with the headland of Devonport and the extinct volcano island of Rangitoto on the horizon. Today was dull, the water choppy. Yet the ozone was like nectar in the air and the cries of the herring gulls, the yachts and craft on the harbour filled Cushla with a nostalgia for Wellington. Though it was all so flat here, without those Wellington hills she'd loved so much. Auckland seemed quite different, sprawling and huge. There were Maoris and Islanders everywhere which Cushla rather liked. They were so much more friendly than Wellington people who could be quite hoity-toity because they lived in the capital where Parliament was. Auckland appeared to be far more modern and there was not so much wind as in Wellington. The Wellington winds had often worn Cushla out, they were so tiring and dried the skin.

Devonport was deserted of people but a few shops were open. The Maori ladies gave Cushla directions, told her to have a look at the real flash homes up on the hill behind the shops where you got a beaut view of the harbour. The ladies lived on a marae, a Maori place in South Auckland, and were visiting relatives here on the North Shore. Cushla felt a bit flat when they said hooray and climbed on board a bus to take them to where they were going. How they'd made her laugh! One of the two made Cushla a present of a large flax basket. They'd admired her flax hat. Cushla was so taken she got a bit teary after they'd gone and Colin began to sling off. Billy was very quiet. He kept staring away from them, walking apart, wouldn't put his arm through hers as Colin did, hiking up the steep street towards a lookout Colin had spotted on the hill. Cushla began to get wheezy halfway up so they had a rest on a park bench beneath some cabbage trees. The sun came out then, piercing the cloud, brightness spreading across the harbour now far below them, causing them to fall silent. Colin had been chatting away to her about his job and the blokes he worked with. The view was quite breathtaking, the distant skyline of the city impressive with the tall buildings and further inland the various cones, the extinct volcanoes Auckland was built round.

'Boy, it's sure a snazzy place, this Auckland,' Colin kept saying, over and over again, until Cushla began to laugh and hug him to her. Billy was sitting at the other end of the park bench, looking upward towards the top of the hill, across his face an expression Cushla couldn't fathom. It made her nervy.

On the way down Cushla bought three double Hokey Pokey ice creams and they headed towards the beach peering into the shop windows on the way, Billy trailing after them acting as if he wasn't there at all. Cushla reckoned he'd got the pip over something and was best left alone, he'd snap out of it. He was acting pretty cranky lately. She'd noticed it since that day he'd been dressed up, reckoned that deep down he missed Seddon a heck of a lot but wouldn't say. She could sense it in his eyes sometimes, the way he stared off in a bit of a dream when he wasn't burying his nose in a book. A real little bookworm now he was at the grammar school.

They settled on the narrow strip of beach near the Devonport ferry building. Cushla laid out the food on serviettes, decided to throw away her old shopping bag and use the new flax one she'd been given, got Colin to turf the old bag into a rubbish bin. She suggested they have a paddle before lunch. She'd brought a towel so they could wipe their feet after.

'Nah, I don't want to, Mum, the sea's too cold,' Colin said, grinning at her. 'Bet you will, though. What about you, Billy? I'll watch the grub!'

Billy shook his head. He was glancing away along the beach, to where two young blokes in swim togs were sitting on a stone wall, watching him. Cushla thought she'd seen them before, on the ferry coming over, but wasn't certain. She took off her shoes and walked carefully down to the edge of the water, looking for pretty shells she could take home and put along the edge of the small garden at the flat. She avoided the stranded jellyfish and the seaweed before stepping into the water. It was freezing cold but it eased her aching corns. Holding up the hem of her frock, she looked back to the boys expecting them to sling off and make jokes about her legs, ready to laugh. Colin was opening the bottles of fizz and wasn't looking her way. Billy had turned his back to his brother, was now staring openly at the two young blokes along the beach who were grinning and saying things to each other. They were looking at Billy so strangely it brought back to Cushla with a jolt the strangeness of that afternoon, that awful tittering woman, Phoebe Croft, their discovering Billy dressed up with make-up on his face. She'd no idea why the memory should hit her now; it was something peculiar in those young blokes' faces. Something she couldn't quite put her finger on. She'd been trying to forget about what had gone on at the flat, pretend it hadn't happened at all. She hadn't told Colin, pushed it to the back of her mind, until this minute.

Billy had begun to tremble a bit, sitting there on the sand. He had first seen the two blokes on the ferry and they'd stared and stared at his legs, their eyes travelling over his body in a way which had made his heart thud with a kind of excitement that had given him a headache. The two blokes had stayed on the beach while he and Mum and Colin climbed the hill. Now they grinned at Billy, were talking to each other without taking their gaze off him. Billy found it impossible to look away for more than a minute.

Cushla had got rid of Phoebe Croft as quickly as she could that afternoon, so shook with embarrassment she couldn't now remember what she'd said to the woman. Those tiny black, beady eyes had been everywhere. In the woman's manner as she'd left had been a kind of delirious urgency. Cushla had no doubt that the news would be gossiped all over church, and that Restel might hear of it. Billy had admitted that someone had been knocking on the front door before she'd got back. He and Martin had hidden in the hall until whoever it was had gone away. Said that the person had tried to peer in through a gap at the edge of the blinds and tapped on the window, calling out, 'Yoo hoo, anyone at home?' It had been Phoebe Croft, Cushla was certain. The woman didn't even live in the district either, so she'd gone out of her way to be nosey. It shook Cushla, that. As if the woman had been sent to spy on her.

Billy looked away in sudden panic as the two blokes jumped down from the wall. He thought they were coming over to speak. One of them, a Maori not much older than Seddon, gave a wave and a huge grin as they moved off up across the grass towards the road. Billy watched until the pair of them disappeared into a milk bar. They kept looking over their shoulders at him, still grinning, their eyes on Billy revealing more than mere friendliness.

Colin suddenly said, 'Who're those jokers? Do you know them?' and Billy shook his head, his face growing scarlet, unable to look Colin in the face, staring down at his feet. Colin threw a handful of sand at Billy, then laughed.

Cushla hadn't known what to make of Billy dressing up like a woman. The clothes were the ones he'd worn for the Cinderella skit, he'd told her. He and Martin had just been having a bit of fun after school, he'd said. Cushla had been more shook at Martin smoking a cigarette, when she'd thought about it. She'd sent Martin home after having a go at him. Made Billy take the clothes off straight away and scrub his face with hot water and soap until all trace of the caked-on make-up had gone, felt like laughing out loud one minute and so wild at him the next. Hiding the clothes and the wig and sending him to bed before Colin came home from work. She'd been terrified he'd see Billy dressed up. Her head had been in a whirl; sitting down at the kitchen table with a cuppa, her hands started to tremble from queer thoughts. She worried herself sick for days that someone from the church might knock on the door. No one came. Nobody arrived to collect her for the working bee, as far as she could tell when she got home that day. She spent the time walking down to her job so nervous in case she should see that Phoebe Croft woman again, not able to say anything to Billy as Colin was about most of the time. Billy stared at her, expecting words. She could not, would not tell Colin about it for fear of what he would say, or might do. She reckoned he didn't like Billy much. Colin was a deep sort. She could never fathom him out. He kept to himself and rarely talked to her. He just liked to get on with his life.

Billy kept looking back towards the milk bar. Colin watched him out of the corner of his eye. Billy was agitated. He stood up once and brushed sand from the seat of his shorts then sat down again suddenly, staring out at the yachts in the harbour with an air of concentration, sipping from his bottle of fizz, all the while taking short, furtive glances over his shoulder. The two blokes did not reappear. Billy seemed unable to sit still.

Cushla spread out a serviette on the sand for her to sit on when she joined them after her paddle, drying her feet and showing the boys the shells she'd collected, handing out the food, making a fuss to cover her uneasiness at Billy's odd behaviour. She'd watched him, too. As they sat eating in a strained silence, a young couple came down to the beach across the grass with two kiddies in tow. One of the kiddies, such a tiny tyke barely able to walk, eventually tottered over to Billy and stood staring at him, his hands behind his back and an intense gaze on his face. Silently Billy picked up one of the fritters and held it out. The little tyke took it eagerly, stuffing it into his mouth and chewing like the blazes, making each of them start to laugh, and the tension in the air went off somewhere else.

Before long the young couple had joined them, at Cushla's friendly suggestion. She sat chatting away about babies and family while Billy, having finished eating, began to make sandcastles with the two boys, Colin looking with a slight grin on his face. Now it was he who kept glancing towards the milk bar.

A shower of rain forced them from the beach, back to the ferry building. The young couple lived locally and

Cushla had got on so well, had chatted so much she felt anxious now, in case they should be late for the picture show. They waited for ages on the dock for the ferry to appear. The rain stopped only after it had arrived and was chugging back out across the harbour heading to the city wharf. Just before it left Cushla noticed the two young blokes come running through the barrier, leaping on board with seconds to spare, now wearing jeans and Hawaii shirts and sandals. They sat not far away from where Billy remained close to Cushla, staring over at Billy now and then, aware that Cushla was watching them intently, she sensing that Billy was acting very fidgety and nervous. There was something unsettling in the young blokes' eyes. They seemed to leer at Billy. Cushla felt a protectiveness towards Billy which confused her. Each of them remained silent all the way across the choppy water. There was only the five of them on board. The strange tension had come back.

The boys' excitement was muted when Cushla let it out that she was shouting them to a musical picture show she'd heard so much about.

'It's all set in our part of the world,' she told them cheerily, trying to disperse the tension still there between them. 'And it's on a huge screen called Todd something, I know you'll like it!' trying hard to recapture that other, long-ago excitement when she'd taken them to see the Danny Kaye picture in Wellington. As they hurried along Queen Street hot rods and motorbikes were roaring up and down, there were lots more people about, young couples arm in arm window shopping and groups of teenagers standing on the corners, laughing and gay despite the drizzling rain which fell.

Cushla held Billy's hand tightly, urging them on, half-aware that it wasn't merely to get to the theatre quickly but to get away from the two young blokes who had followed, Cushla not looking back after seeing them again as they'd crossed Customs Street at the lights. She glanced at Billy who kept staring straight ahead, his face bright pink. It was a relief when they arrived outside the Plaza, walked into the foyer, buying the tickets and moving with the crowd into the huge interior. They were shown their seats just as the lights dimmed and the wonderful music filled the air. As the curtain rose revealing an enormous screen, the sight took Cushla's breath away and totally captured both Billy and Colin's attention, flinging them into a world which caused Cushla's spirits to soar and the boys' faces to shine in the darkness, with the thrill of it and the colour. Cushla was totally transported by the romance between the handsome brute of a Frenchman and the gorgeous American girl. And all those beefy sailors! The music filled her heart. She wept buckets at the end, like the Maori lady had reckoned she might.

Billy was beaming all over his face as they came out into the late afternoon sunshine. The rain had stopped and the tarmac was steaming as they crossed Queen Street heading towards the bus stop. Billy talked non-stop about the picture show. Cushla had bought him a souvenir book which was full of bright, colourful photos. He kept pointing things out and it was a heck of a job to keep him from bumping into people, as the streets were chock-a-block. He was still talking when they clambered onto the trolley bus, found seats at the back, Billy sitting close to Cushla, Colin behind them very quiet but grinning. Billy was leaning against his mum now, telling her there was a long-playing record of all the songs, that the story was from a book and the show had been running at the Plaza for two years and the screen was called Todd A O. Talking in such a loud voice and leaning back to show Colin the pictures in the book half the bus was listening in and trying to have a look as well. An enormously fat lady with five kiddies called out to Cushla that she reckoned she'd have to take her family now or they'd be cranky for a week about it, and everyone else in the bus started to laugh.

It was raining again quite heavily when they stepped off the bus at Mount Albert. Cushla had her brolly in the flax bag and they sheltered beneath it, tramping through puddles and gasping from the sharp wind which had sprung up, blowing the rain into their faces all the way up the avenue. By the time they reached the alley leading down to the flats, they were drenched to the skin but laughing fit to bust and trying to hold each other up. Billy had rolled up his souvenir book and stuffed it inside his shirt to keep it dry. Colin had his arm round Billy's shoulders, Cushla struggling to keep the brolly and her shopping steady, pleased as punch that the picture show had made the boys so much happier with each other. They arrived at the end of the alley to see a car parked there and a man in an oilskin clambering out who Cushla half-recognized. The man's face was so serious, so gloomy it caused the three of them to stop still right there and then.

It was Seddon's boss, from the Morrinsville garage. Seddon was sitting on the porch steps, leaning back against the wall. Billy spotted Seddon first and ran to him with a sharp cry. For a minute or two Cushla couldn't see her oldest boy there, moving past the man as he reached out to grab her arm, suddenly seeing Seddon with such clarity from the light streaming out of the flat next door. Seddon with a horribly swollen jaw and blackened eye and one arm in a sling. Cushla rushed to him herself, to where he sat ignoring Billy entirely, staring at the wall in front of him. Seddon looked so crook! Struggling to his feet as she approached him, his eyes glazed with exhaustion and what Cushla thought was pain. Then his tripping on the step and falling, falling down onto her garden made her cry out.

Cushla had Seddon indoors and on the settee with a blanket over him before she remembered the man, Seddon's boss. He was still outside on the porch, uncertain about entering. She made a pot of tea after bringing him indoors and apologizing, hardly even remembering his name. Having to ask as he took off his coat and sat down with her at the kitchen table a while later. Seddon was sleeping, not having said a word to anyone. He was so pale. Billy knelt on the floor beside his brother, holding Seddon's arm with a look of panic on his face.

Melvin and a gang of his rough mates had cornered Seddon one night outside the garage where he was working late down at Morrinsville, and beat him up so badly Seddon had stitches in his arm from a knife cut and was bruised all over, including his face. His boss, Mr King, had found Seddon outside their house to where he'd crawled home and collapsed against the paling fence. Him and his wife had rushed Seddon to hospital where he'd been kept for two days. Cushla got so wild no one had contacted her but, as Mr King pointed out, there was no telephone here. It was thought better that he should drive Seddon up to Auckland as soon as Seddon was well enough for the trip. He was all right now, Mr King told her, just pretty shook up. When Cushla asked why on earth Melvin had done it when he and Seddon had been such good mates in the past, Mr King fell silent and hung his head, looking dreadfully embarrassed. He made his excuses soon after without explaining a thing, insisted that he had to get going, it was a long drive back and he didn't want to leave his wife alone half the night. Cushla thanked him so many times on the way out to the car it made Mr King's face grow red. Before driving off he handed Cushla a sealed envelope with her name on it, not meeting her eyes.

'It's from Tony Young,' he told her. 'Asked me to make sure you got the letter and not your husband, it explains everything,' getting into his car quickly then, backing out along the alley, not looking at Cushla even when she waved and called out for him to drive safely.

Back inside the flat, staring at Seddon's swollen sleeping face, Billy almost in tears there beside him, both Billy and Colin firing questions at her, as frantic as she, Cushla felt her head would explode. She just had to get out into the fresh air again.

Clutching the letter from Mr Young against her bosom she hurried back and forth along the alley in the darkness and the rain, looking for Restel who she knew wouldn't appear; things just didn't happen like that. Looking for him anyway, pushing the sight of Seddon from her mind, angry at the rain, angry at the wind and her stupid brolly which kept collapsing. Aiming the anger anywhere to avoid the thought of Seddon's attackers and what had been done to him. Almost crushing the letter from Mr Young to her bosom she shook with worry, there in the rain-drenched dark.

Keeping the Peace with Silence

Sometime after Seddon had been brought up from Morrinsville and after Restel had eventually returned from Bulla's funeral they shifted from the flat to a rented house at Onehunga, a suburb further south from the city whose Maori name meant, in translation, 'the place of burial'. Restel had been left money in Bulla's will. Suddenly they were well off, or so Cushla thought.

Dear Cushla Bevan,

I've asked Doyly King if he will hand this letter to you when he gets your boy up to Auckland and to make certain Restel doesn't see it. I reckoned you wouldn't fret over that. You and me got on real well down here and I've no grudge against you about the job. So I wanted to explain about your boy getting beaten up. I reckon it was partly my fault for letting out something I should have kept my mouth shut over.

I never really understood what was going on that day in the bush when I saw your boys and you. I saw but didn't make sense of it. It made me feel too crook. What made it worse was seeing your face, the look on your face. And I'm blowed that I let it all out, you see, to Lynette a couple of weeks back. Lynette gossiped and I'm pretty certain that Melvin heard about it and that's the reason he beat Seddon up, goaded on by his mates. He's a nasty bugger, that boy, and I know what I'd do to him. I still can't say for certain but I reckon that's what happened. We had it hushed up from the coppers, so no worries there.

You are a fine handsome woman, Cushla, and it was hard for me not to come over to say hooray before you left. I have you in my heart. I reckon you knew that. I don't reckon we'll meet again but you hold your head up high and keep smiling. Your smiling reached out to me.

Tony Young

Cushla became quite shaky the first time she had read the letter, sitting on the back step back at the flat in Mount Albert. She was astonished how well written the letter was, the beauty of his words. She'd read the letter numberless times since then, and now they'd shifted to Onehunga. Now the letter was creased and finger-stained, hidden deep in her dresser. She had kept quiet about it. Told no one. The reason why Seddon had been so brutally bashed up hadn't really been a shock, however upsetting was the knowing that Billy and Seddon having been filthy and drunk in the bush was being yakked about by people down there. It was human nature to gossip, she supposed. It was Mr Young's words at the close of the letter which made her return to it again and again in the following months. Reading the letter when alone and away from Restel and the boys, lingering over Mr Young's words. Knowing that he too had felt desires as she had felt them. He hadn't been able to show anything either but it was there, revealed now, directed at her heart. She'd thought about writing back for so long it was now too late and would only have added to the guilt she tried to shove aside. All the while as the months went by she'd had dreams about him. Waking up in a cold sweat to see Restel beside her in the bed, having him ignore her body as if it didn't exist. The feelings receded only because of the disruptions and pressures of their shifting to the large three-bedroomed house in Onehunga. They were renting it, for very little, with some of the money Bulla had left Restel in her will.

127

Restel had returned to the flat at Mount Albert from Wellington busting with the news, acting almost as if his sister was still alive and not dead before her time. He'd been filled with plans to have a house built on new land going cheap out at South Auckland, where a large number of new Aucklanders were heading. Cushla felt a bit revolted by his behaviour, so soon after his sister's death. She was sick to death of hearing about it. As if Seddon being brutally bashed up didn't matter. That Billy doing so well at the grammar school and his winning prizes for his poems had nothing to do with Restel and his plans for their future. That Colin's steady apprenticeship to be a carpenter being disrupted with more shifting was not important either. Restel charged into his plans like a bull at a gate and Cushla had hardly time to blink before they had moved to this house in Onehunga. The packing and arranging were like dreary tasks they'd all become too familiar with. No excitement at seeing the house, no excitement at new prospects in the future. All except for Restel who was full to the brim with plans and thanking the Lord in every second breath, insisting they attend church in town, sometimes twice a day on Sundays. Staring at Cushla with pain when she said she was too tired to go during the week. He tried to read to them from the Bible at the table after tea. One night Seddon leaped from his chair with a wild cry and ran off to his room, slamming the door after shouting words Cushla hadn't ever heard before.

Seddon had not found a job until they'd moved to Onehunga. He'd moped about the flat, kept to himself, ignoring Billy; a painful thing for Cushla to see. His wounds healed quickly, after several check-ups at the doctor's, and he had the stitches removed from his arm where it'd been slashed. There was a dreadful scar. He would not talk about what had happened, simply refused to. As far as Cushla knew, he hardly talked to Billy either.

He seemed a little pally with Colin. They'd tinker with the Chrysler quite a lot and talk together out front.

Cushla had finished up at her Mount Albert job the day after Seddon had been brought home by Mr King. She'd popped down to the office the following morning, explained as best she could that one of her boys was crook, that she'd need to be at home to take good care of him. The solicitors hadn't wanted her to go, said they'd keep the job open. But Cushla had been firm, for she thought Restel would be back any day. As it turned out it had been weeks longer before he'd showed up. By that time Seddon was up and about, going off on long walks during the daylight, silent and depressed. Cushla had left him alone, trusting he'd snap out of it sooner or later.

Seddon began to sling off and make cracks after they'd moved to Onehunga. It was a good sign that he was better. Cracking on about their old heap of a car parked in the drive looking like a real jalopy and next door, where the owners' huge, flash house overlooked theirs, the three shiny and new cars always parked there. It was the only time, though, during that period that Cushla had seen Seddon's old self emerge. Attempting to make them laugh. The owners had parties every Saturday night round a lit-up swimming pool out the back next door. Their two-storied house overlooked quite a lot, as the road was very steep. Despite a large orchard and a high hedge round the back yard, Cushla was often aware of watching eyes whenever she was hanging out the washing.

The shift had happened so fast Cushla had little time to think, and the events while Restel had been away were mostly brushed aside because of Restel's plans. He'd continued with his clerking job in town saying he'd find a job locally when their own home was built. Cushla had

lost count of how many jobs Restel'd had. She had kept
quiet about things, of course, not knowing if Restel knew
anything about why Seddon had been beaten up. He
didn't ask her one question about it. Yet she had kept her
mouth shut too. Cushla did not wear lipstick now or her
new frock. She made certain Billy took all the fancy
dressing-up clothes back to school. Restel told her little
about Bulla's funeral but she could see in his face that her
death had taken its toll.

'The Lord looks after His own,' Restel was fond of
stating. 'I've prayed for us and He has heard. The Lord
moves in mysterious ways. We're meant to have a house
built, with His blessing.' Words like those had begun to
grate on Cushla's nerves. She felt herself cringing every
time she heard him speak that way now. She kept her
mouth shut to keep the peace, and because, like Restel,
she had so little, at this time, to say. They stared at each
other more than they spoke, with pain in their eyes.

They had been living in the rented house for some time
and Billy had been travelling into town on a diesel bus,
then catching a trolley out to Mount Albert where he
continued at the grammar. He came home late every day,
exhausted but determined to carry on with his learning.
Restel hardly made any comment about that for quite a
while, although he'd mentioned to Cushla that Billy was
old enough now to get out to work. Colin still worked at
Mount Roskill, getting a lift there from one of the blokes
he was friendly with. Restel told them he'd worked out a
system whereby Seddon and Colin would provide money
from their pay packets towards rising costs and the new
house, far and above the money they should have been
paying for board, in Cushla's opinion. Seddon did his
block about the plan to Cushla, on the quiet.

'He wants us to have a home,' Cushla told Seddon.
'We've never had a real one, never, not one we'll own. Go

130

along with it, son, please, there's a good boy. We must keep the peace!'

'He's rolling in money now. I know it!' Seddon said. 'Mean old basket.'

Seddon said nothing more but Cushla could see an anger building up inside him. A few days after that he brought home a second-hand Austin car he'd splashed out on with his savings. Restel was livid, shouted at him about wasting money; they had a car. Cushla had never heard him shout at Seddon before. Seddon quite simply ignored his dad. He kept the car and was now busy doing it up. He went off in it after tea some nights, driving goodness knows where. Often he took Colin with him, never Billy. Seddon went out of his way to avoid Billy, would stare at him with a kind of fear in his eyes. Billy would look back with what Cushla saw as confusion, staring at the ugly scar along Seddon's arm. Restel couldn't help but notice. Cushla waited for him to say something, was disturbed when he didn't.

She kept herself busy during those months, making plans for her new home, her first real home, a bit excited about it on the quiet. Thinking about curtains and carpets and colours even though the house wasn't yet built. She had to keep cheery, she thought. Restel brought home the news one night that he'd put a deposit on a quarter-acre section out at Otahuhu in South Auckland, had been to see a building company which put up houses that had set plans. She'd have to help him pick one out so that he could go ahead with arrangements. Cushla began to panic about money until he let out just how much money Bulla had left him. Seddon had been right, he'd always said Bulla had been worth quite a few bob. Cushla was quite shook over the amount, as well as by the fact which Restel made all too clear, that the money had been left to him and he intended to keep it that way. The house would be in his name, as would be the land and new furniture.

'I can't rely on you,' he told her. 'I've received two

letters this week about you running up bills at Farmer's in town, and another from Whitcombe's. I won't have you squandering again, do you hear me?'

Cushla went beetroot. She'd bought Billy poetry books on the layby and had opened an account at Farmer's Trading while Restel had been away, to get the clothes for her and the boys when they'd still been at Mount Albert. She had forgotten all about it. She'd planned to pay it all off before she'd finished at her job there, which she still thought Restel knew nothing about. In the end, she'd spent everything on shouts and good food and had nothing over and forgot, with Restel shunting them off on another shift. Restel told her he'd been forced to pay off her bills himself.

'From now on you'll be a proper wife,' he told her. 'I'm the breadwinner, that's the way things are meant to be!' He stared at her until she turned away. In his gaze she thought she glimpsed a suspicion of what she had been up to. Her guilt didn't allow her to argue. She felt too worn out lately to object to anything. In her heart there was growing a dread of what was happening. A lack of laughter, an uneasiness since Restel's return from Wellington and his bossiness over them. Just because he now had the money to change things. They all went to church together on Sundays because he willed it but something was slipping away from Restel's grasp and he knew it. The Phoebe Croft woman hadn't said a word about Billy to anyone, thank goodness: the gossip would have got back to Cushla. Instead, she sometimes watched Cushla with a peculiar expression, staring at Billy from a distance with her black beady eyes.

They went out to view the section and meet a bloke from the building company, on a Saturday, Restel insisting they all go as a family. He refused to let Seddon drive his own car. The Chrysler was now in such a state it broke down twice on the Great South Road and backfired so many times Seddon really scoffed about it, causing Restel to get pretty hot under the collar. He said nothing but Cushla felt him fuming beside her on the front seat.

Cushla wasn't all that struck by the section Restel had chosen, along a blind road, merely a packed gravel track at this stage, as rough as roads through the bush down south. Restel stood talking to the man from the builders for ages. Cushla sat in the car with the boys, the doors open. Seddon had cheered up and was making cracks about their being able to keep sheep and a herd of cows in the back yard once Restel's shack was up. They could let chooks run free all over the blinking place. Cushla could have a stall out on the Great South Road and sell the eggs. She could hand out free tracts about how to get saved. Build milking sheds too, as it was defunct farming land. Christians were supposed to build their houses on rock and here they were, having been gypsies for years, building a house on dried-up cow poop. Soon Cushla was laughing so much the tears were pouring down her cheeks. Restel kept looking over, glaring at her as he continued to go on and on to the man from the builders, who looked bored stiff. He went bright pink when Restel handed him some gospel tracts before saying hooray. The bloke drove away quickly not even looking at Restel again. Restel came over and told Cushla that everything was set up. He'd sign all the papers next week and make the payments and it would only be a matter of months before the house would be up and finished so they could shift in. Cushla couldn't credit that it could be done so fast.

On the drive back to Onehunga, Restel told Billy that he would have to leave school at the end of term and find a job. He'd need all the help with money he could get for extras and it was about time Billy was in a job and not wasting his time acting like a pansy at that school. Restel would find Billy a good manly trade to get into. Cushla

133

was shook at the way Restel spoke to Billy, the harshness in his voice. Surely he didn't need more money. Billy had become pretty withdrawn since Seddon's return and now he went pale, and sat staring out the window, unable to speak.

After a while he said in a trembling voice, 'I wanted to get my School Cert. and go to university.'

Restel responded angrily, 'You'll do nothing of the sort! Your brothers work and now it's your turn and you can cut out your impudence!'

No one laughed. Seddon didn't make a crack as he would have done years ago. His face was tight, had also paled. The atmosphere inside the car became stifling. Restel began to tear a strip off Billy in a dull, droning tone, about him acting more like a man and toughening himself up and to stop behaving like he didn't belong to them. He was being a real toffee-nosed sissy. Billy said nothing to defend himself. He acted as if he hadn't heard. His face remained drawn, without colour. He kept glancing at Seddon. Seddon stared straight ahead.

They'd only been home a few minutes and Restel was hauling Billy into his bedroom for something he'd muttered. Some dreadful cheek. Restel slammed the door; then came Restel's shouts and the sounds of Billy being beaten for minutes that seemed endless to Cushla. Restel came out to find her there glaring at him from the hallway. She was ready to have a right go at him. Seddon and Colin had gone back outside to Seddon's car. They were revving up its motor and making a real racket out there.

'You will kill me, the way you treat him,' Cushla told Restel in a low voice. 'You call yourself a Christian, beating him like that, you are mental!' But the anger she longed for flew away beneath Restel's gaze. She broke off, moved from him into the kitchen aware of his eyes on her back and shivered at the determined look she had seen in his face.

'Little squirt,' she whispered. 'You wait, you just wait.'

She couldn't go into Billy's room to see if he was all right. She couldn't face it.

Within a month Billy had not only arranged to leave school but was offered a job at the IGA in town. He said nothing about it to any of them, went ahead and looked through the newspaper each day for a job, dealt in his own way with his English master at the grammar, who was convinced Billy should not leave despite him being old enough. Billy and Martin vowed they would keep in touch. Billy remained calm, on the surface.

He was growing slowly aware of being different. Having been told so many times he was special, he was moved to strive harder to achieve, without thinking about it, aware that for some reason he had to prove something. Already he felt apart from his brothers. He thought he was learning to accept that, in his own thoughts and ways. Seddon's ignoring him, looking at him with the expression of not wishing Billy to be there because of what had gone on between them, caused Billy's isolation to become real. It became a part of his life then. He thought the others didn't really give a hoot anyway. Everything went along as it always had. The distancing did scare him for he did not fully know its cause. He hadn't talked about it to anyone. It was something unspoken. Although so real it made him withdraw into a private world where books and poetry became a shelter. He said nothing about leaving school and arranging an interview for a job until he'd been offered the job and was in his last weeks at school. Told his dad at the tea table, his mum sitting there watching him with a trembling of her lips. Billy told them with a bit of pride in his voice. Restel's reaction was unexpected. Billy even told them what day he was to start and what the job entailed. It was just a general job, delivering parcels with the prospect of being trained on a course for commercial art, as the company handled advertising for a large New Zealand grocery chain. He expected Restel to be pleased and asked for a confirming letter to be sent to school as they needed it.

Restel's reaction was a mixture of surprise and angry bluster. He felt insulted that Billy had gone ahead without saying a word, picking a job he'd sought out himself. It shook Restel, deepened his developing worry over Billy's behaviour. Between them there now arose an awareness of that, what Cushla reckoned was stupid pig-headedness. A clash of wills, without it being spoken of. A silent yet cutting contest between them which caused Cushla to fret and Colin and Seddon to pull away from Billy all the more. They didn't want to know what was going on. For Seddon the guilt he felt made his rejection of Billy even sharper than it might have been. Colin just said nothing, as usual.

Restel now began to watch Billy, to question everything he did.

In leaving school because he had no choice, in finding himself a job without help, Billy changed, suddenly. He found what seemed to be a strange kind of strength, however tenuous it would prove to be. It threw Cushla into a panic, during those months as work on the house out at Otahuhu began and Restel's attitude towards Billy became more and more dictatorial. Yet too much time had gone by. Too much had happened that no one mentioned. Even Billy was not a kiddy anymore. Cushla watched him and his dad moving further and further apart, both of them staring back over their shoulders with looks Cushla couldn't fathom, looks which made her tremble.

Billy did begin to act a bit more cheery and confident. He went about the house in Onehunga with a light step. Refused to go out to the section at Otahuhu with his dad and brothers to help clear the scrub from it. He did so one time and came home crying, then hid in his room. Cushla overheard Restel telling Colin that Billy was useless. Cushla reckoned that Restel didn't know what to do. He behaved as if Billy was defying his will. He more or less told Cushla that as they lay in bed at night, neither able to sleep, Cushla silent, Restel going on and on and blaming it all on Billy not having come to the Lord to be saved and what he'd have to do about that. Both Seddon and Colin had been born again now. Colin had been a witness for the Lord at Sunday church, as Seddon once had. Restel had given Colin a new leather-bound Bible, some money and a toolbox for work.

'You told Billy to go and get a job, you told him! What on earth do you expect?' Cushla hissed one night, having heard enough of his ranting. Restel glared at her, just as he always did when she argued at something he'd say. At least it shut him up then, Cushla thought, when she answered him back. She was sick to death of hearing him going on like a wound-up gramophone because he was head of the house.

She kept remembering Kitty's words, so long ago. About the tribulations a man like Restel would bring. She often thought of Kitty and Radley. They were lost to each other now. No one wrote or contacted the others.

'Little squirt,' she whispered into the darkness at Restel when she thought he was asleep.

Each of the boys was finding wings. They might soon fly away, or attempt to. Billy, however, seemed to be facing a different direction. She feared Restel was aware of that, as she was aware of it in her heart, and it frightened her. Restel was waiting. He was waiting and watching Billy with the steady gaze of a hawk in the sky.

With Threat of Stormy Weather

The building of the new house went on and on, an endless thing for Cushla as the months slowly turned. So much time had gone by, she kept thinking. Now her boys were almost adults. Where had that begun?

A damp chill developed in the air and a ludicrous tension lingered and grew in the house at Onehunga, like a cloud. It was only a few weeks now before they were to shift, and Cushla had begun packing. A lot of things they were dumping out at a tip in Mangere, buying new.

Restel travelled to and from the section as often as his free time permitted, keeping an eye on things. Colin often went with him. Told Cushla that Restel was being a real pong up the builders' noses.

'He goes on about how they should be doing things,' Colin said to Cushla one night. 'Boy, it's a fluke they don't bash him one, they must get so brassed off!'

Heavy rain held things up. Cushla was shook how those delays touched Restel. It put him into a real foul mood and she tried to keep out of his way. Seddon cracked on that he was in a hurry to shift them all to the house so he could play Moses.

'There's no need to sling off,' Cushla snapped. 'He's doing his best!'

In her gaze Seddon's face went beetroot. He was reminded of what he'd done on the farm whenever Cushla stared at him. He didn't say anything more. Cushla took to spending time, when Restel was home, out the back weeding the vegetables she'd planted and sitting on the rickety wooden bench under a pear tree, finding some peace and breathing in the sweet air. She had not gone out to the house yet with Restel, as Colin and Seddon had, saying to Restel she only wanted to see it when it was nearly finished. It'd mean more to her then. The way each of them was carrying on lately spoilt her excitement over their new home, although she did have curtains ready for the kitchen and the bathroom. Restel had brought home the measurements. Her old treadle Singer machine never failed her. It was always the same despite having had a few new parts along the years. The Singer had been a wedding present from her own mum, a link to a long-gone past becoming more and more real in memory, comforting her lately. There was a hope inside her heart that the new house would bring some contentment and calm. Yet that hope seemed real only when she was alone there in the back yard beneath the pear tree. Inside the house Restel and Billy were acting like cranky little boys. She felt like knocking their heads together some mornings after a good night's sleep. By night time she was so worn out the fear and anxiety came, with the dark. She found herself having a weep at such odd moments. Her waterworks seemed to have a mind of their own.

Billy had begun his job at the IGA a while back and had already given Cushla some money for his board and told her he was saving up to buy a push-bike. Cushla had lied to Restel about how much Billy was giving her. He'd reckoned Billy should pay as much as his brothers, even though Billy earned far less. Cushla told Billy to keep quiet about the amount he gave her each week.

Every Saturday morning Restel hauled Billy out of bed at six o'clock without fail, getting on Cushla's nerves. It was stupid.

'We all have to muck in,' Restel told her. 'I'm not having him lazing about!'

He would drive off out to the section after that, in the Chrysler. Cushla would let Billy go back to bed as soon as Restel had gone and they'd had breakfast. Colin went out with Restel to help. They were building a shed on the section to keep their tools dry. Seddon would sometimes join Cushla and Billy for breakfast. Cushla tried her darnedest to get them to talk to each other, yet in front of her they just acted shifty. Seddon worked all day on Saturdays, and Cushla would find herself alone before the morning had gone. Billy would go off into town. He told Cushla he went to the pictures and rode on the ferry boat to Devonport and back.

'Don't you let on to your dad,' Cushla warned him. 'He keeps asking what you get up to, all the time.' It made her so crook in her heart when her eyes met Billy's. Restel forcing him to leave school like that. It wasn't right.

'I don't mind, Mum,' was all Billy would say when she spoke to him. Yet his eyes betrayed him, and his expression grabbed Cushla's heart and squeezed it.

One evening near tea time when Billy came home from work later than usual Restel was in Billy's room going through his things. Billy stood in the doorway staring. Restel had taken all Billy's poems out from his tallboy and had ripped them up. He was examining Billy's library books and a notebook he kept hidden under his mattress. Billy backed away from the door. Restel didn't even notice him there. Cushla was in the kitchen, getting tea. She was singing a hymn and banging plates about. Billy reckoned she knew what was going on.

Billy hurried down the hall into his mum and dad's room. Pulling out the drawers of Restel's tallboy he tipped the contents onto the bed. He picked up the bags of boiled lollies Restel kept hidden, took them into the living-room and scattered them all over the floor. Then he ran from the house, walking down towards the Onehunga shops once he was out of sight of the front door, as dusk deepened into night. Sat on a bench to watch the passing traffic. A man in a car drove past three times, slowly. The man stared at Billy with a lecherous gaze. Billy poked his tongue out at the man. After a while he began to giggle and laugh

141

helplessly and to feel angry at the same time and lonely for something he also feared.

Not a word was spoken, when Billy went back. Restel pretended nothing out of the ordinary had gone on. Billy kept the ripped up poems which he rescued from the bin. He put all the pieces together and copied the poems into a book which he began to carry with him in his old school satchel to and from work. The silence was now so heavy it made Cushla wild. She went about the house using the Hoover, bashing the furniture with it and singing hymns at the top of her voice.

Restel confronted Billy the next night with one of his library books, holding it high in the air as Billy had seen him holding his Bible whenever he was preaching.

'You will not read filth!' Restel shouted at Billy. 'It's poisoning your mind, do you know that?' and he slammed the book down on the table, his face livid. Billy stared at the floor. Silently he picked the book up and took it back to his room, closing the door behind him.

Billy went to the library every Friday night when it stayed open late. It stood at the bottom of the road where the shops stretched down the hill towards the Manakau harbour, the southern harbour of Auckland. No one else in the family read except his dad. Restel read travel books and sometimes history. Billy borrowed novels and poetry. From then on Billy hid his library books at the back of his wardrobe, taking the one he was reading with him when he went to his job in town. He read the books on the bus and in his room at night when silence had come and the others were asleep.

Seddon set eyes on Beth for the first time about then, at his job working in a garage at Te Papapa, not far from Onehunga. The garage was small and there was only

Seddon and the owner working there. The pay was poor. Seddon was merely biding time, reckoned he could find a better job in South Auckland once they'd shifted into the new house. Beth came in to get someone to look at her car's muffler which had developed a hole. Seddon's boss fixed the fault himself, going on and on to Seddon about how he could really root that sheila, given the chance.

'Look at those udders on her!' he'd said as Beth was leaving after arranging what had to be done. If she'd heard him she didn't let on. Seddon's new boss was a pretty filthy bloke with a foul mouth. Seddon did his best to put up with it but it really got up his nose, like the bloke's BO did whenever their paths crossed.

Beth had stared at Seddon with a grin on her face and her eyes had travelled across his body slowly, causing Seddon to drop a spanner the first time she did that. Yet she hadn't been poking fun at him, just the opposite, he reckoned. After she'd gone Seddon couldn't stop thinking about her. He thought she was old enough to be his mum and wasn't even good looking. Yet there was something about her, though he couldn't for the life of him just pinpoint what it was. By the end of the day, having slogged his guts out because the boss had shoved off to the boozer, Seddon felt too brassed off to think much about anything.

Restel found a packet of smokes in Billy's work satchel one evening while Billy was helping his mum weed the vegetables out the back. Billy had begun to smoke at work. He kept the cigarette packets and matches rolled up in a sock at the bottom of his satchel. When the two came indoors as darkness was falling, Restel was standing at the kitchen table with the cigarettes held out in his open palm.

'What are these, Billy?' he asked.

'Smokes,' Billy said, his eyes widening.

'How did they get in your room?'

'They're mine,' said Billy. He felt himself beginning to shake. His mouth went dry and he looked over at Cushla. She was standing with her back to the room, peering out the window above the sink. She had moved there as soon as she'd spied Restel's face. Restel screwed up the packet of cigarettes in his hands and threw it at the bin by the door.

'Get to your room,' Restel said.

'I'll lock the door if you come after me,' Billy said before hurrying from the kitchen. Restel followed close behind him. The bedroom door had been pulled to. Over the handle hung the leather braces Restel now used to beat Billy. They'd been put there deliberately. Billy moved into the room. On his bed lay his satchel with its contents scattered. The book he'd copied the poems into was opened but not damaged. Restel, closing the door behind him, said, 'Take your shorts down,' in an angry voice. He began to shout at Billy that smoking was a sin, it was taking in foul substances, poisoning the body which was the Lord's temple. Billy turned to face his dad when he stopped shouting. Billy tried to outstare Restel, then looked away. He was shaking all over.

Restel stepped towards him, raising his right arm, his fist clenching the leather braces. He whipped them down across Billy's shoulders. Billy cried out and backed off. Neither of them spoke. Restel moved closer, raising the braces for a second blow.

It happened so quickly Billy later couldn't credit how he'd managed it, barely remembering what he'd actually done. He pushed Restel away, kicked at him and followed that through with another shove causing Restel to fall. Billy, more scared than angry, ran from the room. Restel was struggling to get up off the floor. Billy ran through the living-room past Cushla, looking stricken, out of the house and down along the street before he stopped and tried to control an overwhelming urge to be sick. Holding his arms across his chest, he stared down at the grass verge until his stomach moved into place and his legs were not like jelly. As he remained standing there quite alone on the street a cold rain began to fall.

Beth kept coming back to the garage where Seddon worked. She'd ask for small adjustments to be made to her car and new parts fitted where there was no need for them. Seddon's boss didn't make any comment as he needed the work, but he reckoned he knew what Beth was up to.

'She wants you to give her a good rooting,' he told Seddon. 'Milk those udders,' and for the first time Seddon told his boss to shut his mouth before he did it with his fist. The old bloke just grinned then kept chuckling for ages, didn't seem at all riled at the way Seddon had spoken.

Seddon and Beth began to talk while she was there. Seddon found that he was quite taken by some of the things she said. She wasn't at all like his boss tried to make out. She was soft and warm and pretty lonely. Though he wasn't all that struck on her looks, within a few days he'd agreed to go to the bach she owned out at Otahuhu for a meal, and she waited for him after work. Seddon's boss said nothing else about her. His eyes watched them as they met outside the garage when Seddon knocked off for the day. They met frequently after that first time. Some days it was bucketing down with rain and Beth waited for him there inside her car. Seddon began to leave his car in the garage and drive off in Beth's. Before long Seddon was dreaming about Beth at night. Thoughts of her made his heart thud like mad. He began to talk more to Billy, began to take notice of what was going on between his brother and Restel and a kind of guilt erupted, a sharp, half-forgotten pain casting a cloud over this need beginning to form for Beth.

Billy was asked to work overtime at his job quite often. He

145

was doing so well there he was told that as the girl who worked the new copying machine was leaving he might take over her job and they'd employ a new message boy. Billy was wasted in his present job, they said. He was bright and would go far. Billy was thankful for the offer, as it meant more money and he'd have his own room in which to work. He booked overtime, making up plates for the printers. One of the printers, Jack Yates, had become friendly towards Billy some time back. The same age as Seddon, Jack was English and known by everyone to be knocking off Raewyn who worked down the hall in accounts and was called a real rooter by the printers as well as by the other women. The other printers slung off at Jack all the time about what he was up to. About what he'd catch off Raewyn if he wasn't too careful, she'd had roots with half the blokes in Auckland. Jack took Raewyn up into the loft every night he worked overtime, told Billy he rooted her on an old mattress on the loft floor. Jack would come into the copyroom after and sit on the table there, talk to Billy about things Billy knew little of. None of them worked that hard, after hours. Jack had been to America and India and reckoned Billy should travel, get away from his useless family. Billy had told Jack quite a lot, but nothing about how he really felt inside. Billy looked at Jack and wanted to ask Jack to touch him, to hold him, even kiss him on the lips. The thoughts terrified Billy. He couldn't tell Jack about that. He was not certain he liked Jack's response to what he did say. Jack made his family sound like they were strangers. He was normally so open about himself Billy felt dishonest, not telling Jack everything, but fear held him back. Yet he showed Jack some of his poems, read a few out to him sometimes at lunch breaks when they were sitting alone on the fire escape high above the city streets. Jack said he thought the poems were fine and that they touched his heart. Billy trembled at that. His mouth went dry and his face burned.

Their friendship deepened, something forming between

146

them which excited Billy. He dreamed about Jack at night. They were odd looking mates. Jack was so tall and dark featured, Billy was so blond and small. Jack would stare into Billy's eyes and cause Billy to feel jittery. He would look for Jack during the day. Their eyes would meet and they would share a secret grin. It was as if Jack knew something about Billy that Billy was not certain he knew about himself. Billy couldn't stop thinking of the moments when he and Jack would be alone together. Began to book in overtime more and more often, as there was plenty of work. Jack did the same, told Billy with that grin of his that he needed the extra money. Billy noticed that Jack had stopped taking Raewyn up to the loft. He'd acted guilty over her when Billy asked questions. Raewyn would come down the hall during the day and stare at Jack where he worked at his machine. Jack would not look up. His face would go bright red. He ignored the laughter the other blokes made, after she'd gone.

For a while, Cushla reckoned that Billy and Restel were keeping out of each other's way on purpose, at home. She breathed a sigh of relief. The tension receded a bit and they seemed a little more taken up with work, with Restel busy on the house being built. Colin went out there far more than any of them except for Restel. He and his dad got on real well. The silence in the house, which was still there, became easier.

Jack took to giving Billy a lift home in his old Morris Minor some nights. Jack lived on the North Shore so it was well out of his way, driving Billy home, but he did it quite cheerfully and became angry when his jalopy of a car played up. Billy reckoned Jack was trying to impress him. They spent more and more time together. Jack was a pretty sad person, underneath the surface of his constant

147

grin. Billy sensed it often, in the looks they swapped. Sometimes Jack would have a hangover in the morning at work. He'd come in to the copy room after Billy started working in there full-time and crawl into the huge cupboards below the equipment to sleep his hangover off. Billy'd pretend he didn't know where Jack was when the supervisor hunted for him. Except for one morning when Jack began snoring just as the supervisor came into the room. Jack got a real telling off but nothing much was said to Billy. Jack said after he was certain he would have got the boot, but hadn't. He was pretty popular round the place and worked hard and cheered everyone up when they were brassed off. The others always went to Jack when they had a moan and he would attempt to sort it out. Billy wished he'd been able to crawl into the cupboards as well with his friend. He reckoned he loved Jack now.

Billy was working overtime on his own one night not long after, apart from some of the commercial artists downstairs. Jack hadn't been needed. About eight o'clock when Billy was tidying up ready to knock off, Jack came in and stood leaning against the doorway.

'I'm a bit shickered, mate,' he said and began to laugh. 'Been down at the Royal. After hours boozing, eh. They reckon I'd make a good barman. I'd take you down there if you weren't so bloody young.' The Royal Hotel was one of Jack's haunts. Both of them, having lit up smokes, stood there and stared at each other. Jack was grinning. All of a sudden he stepped back from the doorway, went about with staggering steps switching off all the lights until it was almost dark. An orange glow came in through the high windows, from the streetlamps outside and the other lights of the city. Threw huge shadows across the floor. Jack walked very slowly back to where Billy waited, standing there with his satchel over his shoulder, ready to leave.

'Aw, struth,' Jack whispered, looking down into Billy's face. Reaching out he pulled the satchel away from Billy, let it fall onto the floor.

148

Jack said, 'I don't reckon you'd . . .' then stopped speaking. He stared into Billy's eyes for a long time. Then he grabbed hold of Billy's arms, pulled Billy to him and kissed him deeply and roughly on the lips, holding Billy against him. Billy struggled and then became still.

Running from Jack down the corridor, leaping down the stairs ignoring the lift, Billy ran all the way to the bus depot once he had got out of the building, not looking back.

The Onehunga bus was there, motor idling, ready to go out.

The driver said, 'Just made it, little mate, hop aboard!' and Billy bought his ticket.

Billy sat on a seat right at the back of the bus unable to stop himself trembling, staring at the floor, not able to raise his sight higher for a while. Frightened that Jack might climb on whenever the bus stopped until it was passing down the Khyber Pass Road and through Newmarket heading south. Seeing that moment when Jack had kissed him like he was viewing some short piece of film again and again, feeling stupid one minute for having run off and glad he had the next. The bus humping and bumping and careering through the dark streets and Billy remembering he'd left his satchel behind and reading the words 'I love big titties' someone had scrawled on the back of the seat in front.

As Billy clambered down off the bus at the top of the road out at Onehunga he didn't see anyone about. He hadn't reckoned he'd see Jack, walked down the steep slope towards the house, unwilling to go home at all, looking up to the sky at stars and wispy cloud and a bright moon.

149

Jack was leaning against his car right outside the house holding up Billy's satchel. He'd driven like the blazes to beat the bus, which hadn't been too difficult once he'd spotted that Billy was on board. Except the car had overheated and steam was now coming up from the bonnet. His face as Billy walked towards him was still. Jack's face looked sad and lonely and nervous at the same time. The car door stood open. After meeting Billy's startled gaze Jack got back onto the front seat and moved over, gesturing for Billy to get in and sit beside him. Billy did, after hesitating for a few minutes, not taking his eyes off Jack, not even looking at the house to see if any lights were on there. Jack leaned across to pull the door shut. Their faces, as he did so, drew close, as close as any two faces could. The full moon, high above them, was shining down.

Neither Billy nor Jack noticed Restel watching the car from the front-room window of the house, just to the left of the porch in the dark. He'd been watching Jack waiting there. He'd seen the car pull up. He'd remained at the window wondering who the stranger was. Restel continued to stare: over his face, revealed by the cold light of the moon, there grew a look of utter revulsion.

A few miles away, not far from the new house going up at Otahuhu, in a small red-roofed bach with a paling fence and two cars parked outside, Seddon and Beth were lying naked on Beth's bed, that same moonlight coming down to touch them through the window. Just as Billy let Jack kiss him again on the lips there in the car Beth was placing her lips gently down over Seddon's cock. Seddon cried out with a frightened joy there on the bed below the wide open window. His voice, drifting upward towards the sky, exposed an overwhelming remembrance of guilt, as well as this feeling inside his heart that Beth had reckoned earlier could be love.

150

Part Four

The toetoe sways and snaps
in the wind.
I hang my head
and weep.
No one seems to hear the same
music.

Billy Bevan

Darkness, Coming down the Road

Tension covered them like a dust by the time they'd shifted into the new house at Otahuhu and been there for some months.

Looking back Cushla wondered how she'd come through those months without going stark, staring mad. Restel acted as if the house itself would be their salvation. That because it was a new house and they'd joined a modern new church at Papatoetoe each of them could become the kind of Christians Restel demanded they should be.

His attitude towards Billy had changed course. Something had gone on back at Onehunga she didn't know about, for it was just before they'd shifted when Restel's cold pretence that Billy didn't really exist except to be punished began to surface. Of course, the shift for each of them had been a heck of a strained time by itself. Little had gone right. The huge lorry Restel had hired and drove himself broke down. A lot of Cushla's crockery had been broken on the trip and Restel had driven the lorry into a ditch along the Great South Road. Seddon had slung off so much Restel had lost his temper and shouted at him. Seddon had gone off in a huff, didn't come back until after dark when most of the furniture and packing cases had been stacked up on the front porch. Restel had covered it all with a tarpaulin but it bucketed down with heavy rain all that night. When Cushla looked out in the morning the packing cases were half-filled with rainwater and the furniture there was soaked through.

'Serves him right for being such a skinflint,' Seddon

scoffed when he joined her. Cushla began to weep from tiredness. Red-faced, Seddon helped to sort out the mess. It'd been Sunday morning, with Restel gone off to morning church so silent and put out that Cushla had refused to go. She'd told him there was far too much to do. By the time he came back, everything was indoors drying out in front of the new electric heaters.

It'd been the worst shift they'd ever had. Their first few weeks in the house caused tempers to flare while the rain continued to fall outside. Restel had found a new job as well as Seddon. Billy and Colin stayed put in the jobs they already had. Cushla was grateful for their working. It helped to smooth over the effects of the upheaval. At least jobs were plenty and they would not starve even if Restel didn't stay at his for long, which was quite likely. Cushla kept forgetting they were now well off but Restel, as he'd told her, kept it to himself. Spare money, for Cushla, was tight. She had decided privately early on to look for a full-time job, would not tell Restel until she was offered one. She had a reference from her temporary employers at Mount Albert. That should almost guarantee something. She began to scan the newspaper, looking for hours that would suit her and good money.

Restel demanded they all go to worship every Sunday morning after that one time Cushla refused to go, insisted then on the boys going to local Youth for Jesus rallies and that Colin and Seddon go with him to rugby matches on Saturday afternoons. In ordering them, he would ignore Billy totally. He'd pretend that Billy was not even in the same room. Seddon and Colin listened to their dad in silence. Colin would obey Restel, Cushla begging him to, just to keep the peace. Seddon told Cushla that Restel could go and get stuffed. Seddon was old enough now to do what he liked.

Billy cleared out of the house very early some Saturday mornings, believing he wasn't wanted there. He caught the bus into town, not coming home until tea at five

154

o'clock. When he began to do that regularly Restel gave him a beating when he came back, without saying why. He had bought a thick leather belt, showed Cushla where he kept it hidden in his tallboy and suggested she also use it if he wasn't home. The belt was three inches wide with a heavy metal buckle. Billy didn't fight back. He submitted to the punishment in complete silence.

'You're vicious,' Cushla hissed at Restel one night. 'Vicious! You are destroying his cheerfulness, you know that? Who do you think you are, eh? You're not God!'

Restel would stare back at her when she spoke like that, as if she hadn't said a word. He would storm off out the back. He'd had a prefabricated garage put up and inside, at the far end, was building a darkroom for his photography. Seddon told Cushla that the timber he was using for the darkroom was riddled with woodworm. With any luck the whole thing would fall on top of him before too long.

'You shouldn't scoff!' Colin butted in, having overheard. 'He's our dad, Seddon!'

Billy watched such scenes, keeping his distance. He had become more secretive than Cushla had ever seen him. He was quiet and withdrawn, putting up with his dad's attitude without saying a word to Cushla about it, nor trying to get his own back as he'd tried to do at Onehunga. He acted depressed. Cushla's heart went out to him whenever Restel beat him with the belt. It was almost the only time Restel had anything directly to do with Billy. He did not speak to him at the tea table but stared through him with coldness. Somehow that was worse than anything else and it had its effect. Billy moved about the house as if he was a shadow. Restel had stopped him from working overtime. Gave Billy times by which he had to be home after work during the week. He would barge into Billy's room at odd moments and sort through his things when Billy wasn't there and even when he was. Cushla checked, one time after Restel had been rummaging,

155

before Billy came home from work. Restel had left everything all over the place, so Billy would know. Cushla fretted and grew angry and wanted to say something or do something but kept her mouth shut and just watched it going on, feeling like a coward. They sat beside each other in church on Sunday mornings and afterwards Restel would speak about the love of Christ and a world out there filled with sinners and damnation. But Cushla knew that his ranting was directed only at her.

Billy had not seen Jack since they'd shifted. A few days before the shift to Otahuhu Jack had disappeared, hadn't come into work and hadn't called in sick. Billy didn't say much, or ask too many questions of the others. Yet he didn't think anyone else knew any more than he did. Jack and Billy having been together so much, the gap it left in Billy's days became like a dark hole. With what went on at home, the way his dad was acting, Seddon still acting shifty with him and Cushla on the surface acting as if nothing was wrong, he just tried to get through each day hoping the next would be better. Looking for Jack all over town in his lunchbreaks. Watching from the bus on his journey home after work, hoping he'd catch a glimpse. The supervisor at work was as stumped as anyone and after two weeks stopped Jack's pay packets and hired someone else, a big burly bloke who swore a lot and boozed even more.

One Saturday morning a postcard arrived from Australia. Billy saw it before anyone else and quickly stuffed it inside his shirt, going back into the house. Shut in his room he took the postcard out with trembling fingers. It was from Jack. He'd known straight away somehow, knew it was without even looking. There were two lines of writing on the back, with Jack's signature and three X's.

Should've taken you with me, little mate. You'd be better off over here, we'd have grand times. Sorry I left without goodbye.

Yours,

Jack.

Billy stared at the words until his sight blurred. He hid the postcard carefully. Stashing his cigarettes in his jacket pocket he went back out to the kitchen. Cushla was at the ironing-board, a huge pile of clothes beside her. She didn't look up.

'I'm going into town,' Billy told her quietly.

'Your dad's down the section. Don't let him see you,' she answered. Billy shrugged. As he went to open the back door she raised her sight and said, 'Billy?' in almost a whisper. Her face was twisted into a kind of smile.

'I love you, son,' she told him. 'You know that, don't you? You remember how much? You're my special . . .' and her voice faltered as her gaze jerked away. Billy didn't answer her. He was shaking like a leaf when he stepped out onto the porch. She had not talked to him like that for a long time. He felt guilty.

Restel glanced up from where he was marking out a vegie garden down the back. His and Billy's eyes met. After a few minutes, Billy walked down across the sprouting grass, drawn by something in Restel's face.

'I could give you a hand if you like, Dad,' Billy suggested.

When Restel didn't reply, didn't look up again but continued to dig the earth as if he hadn't heard, Billy said, 'Dad? Do you want a hand?'

Restel stopped digging. He looked up and away from Billy to the house next door.

'I don't want your help. You're not my son. You revolt me,' he said. Then he turned his back and shoved the spade into the ground. Billy stood staring at his dad's

157

back for a long time. As he turned away and began to run back up across the grass towards the road, he spotted Cushla watching from the kitchen window.

Billy ran all the way to the bus stop feeling that his face was on fire.

Seddon and Beth went to the Deluxe picture house in Otahuhu some evenings. Beth would cook a meal out at her bach, then they'd drive to the main street to see if there was a good film showing. Not that it mattered: it was a cheap night out and they both enjoyed themselves there in the darkness, close and warm together. Beth preferred a good comedy, enjoyed laughing with Seddon as he enjoyed watching and listening to her laughter, which bubbled up as if from a well. The laughter drew them close, in those early days. Seddon was aware that Beth was becoming someone important in his life. The tensions back at the house faded, grew less real the more he was in Beth's company. He tried to forget what was going on between Restel and Billy. Managed to, when he was alone with Beth. They never discussed his family as they rarely discussed hers. Beth's past had been pretty dreadful and she only wanted to forget it. Yet she was tough and almost twice Seddon's age and through that was able to offer Seddon a certain comfort he'd never known before.

They were sitting in the middle stalls of the Deluxe one night watching a Doris Day picture when Seddon happened to glance round. He spotted Colin with a girl he'd not seen about Otahuhu before. She was a Maori, or an islander. Both Colin and Seddon went beetroot when they saw each other. Then they laughed. Beth and Colin's dates stared at each other.

Seddon took Beth out the side door when the picture show was over.

*

Restel arranged for a group of church-goers to visit the new house for a prayer meeting. He told Cushla the night before and she flew into a panic, having little food in the house to offer. With most of her crockery cracked or broken from the shift she had to make do, all the more determined to find a job so she could buy what she wanted. She'd applied for two jobs and was waiting to hear through the post if she was to be given an interview. She had kept quiet about it.

When the visitors arrived in cars and on foot Cushla showed them into the living-room, relieved that both Colin and Seddon were out, away from it. Restel had insisted the two be there, only them, had told Billy he was to stay in his room with the door shut. He didn't want him at the meeting. Colin and Seddon both ignored their dad and shot off out straight after tea.

Cushla remained mostly in the kitchen, fussing over pots of tea and biscuits to hide her irritation, not apologizing when she handed round the meagre refreshments. Now, because she rarely went with Restel to church, some of the visitors stared at her as if she was a stranger. A few of the women got Cushla's ire up from the expressions on their faces. She could not believe they were Christian, not in the way she understood it.

When Restel began to rant on about his backsliding sons and how he and the others there might go about getting them back to the fold, Cushla froze, listening from the kitchen with the sliding doors half-shut. When it became a general discussion, Cushla went to the doors and stood there, staring in. Immediately everyone fell silent and several of the visitors looked at Cushla as if she had no right to be there. Restel started clearing his throat and his face went pink. Cushla was glaring round the room without realizing it. She stepped back into the kitchen and pulled the doors shut. After a few minutes she heard Restel's voice, then one of the old boys, praying. He

159

was praying for her sons, loudly, mentioning each of them by name, spouting sin and redemption in the same breath. When the same old boy started off praying for Cushla's soul, it was the last straw. She jerked up from the table where she'd sat down, rushed over to the doors and slid them open with such force that one almost flew off its rail.

At first she asked politely that they all leave. She said she was feeling crook. When Restel told her in no uncertain terms to leave the room as she was interrupting, she became so riled she lost her temper and was almost shouting for several minutes before storming right through the group and out the other doorway into the hall. Having made it pretty plain just what she thought, not knowing why she was carrying on in such a paddy, saying words which later, when she remembered, she went beetroot over. Charging up the narrow hall to her room, seeing Billy in his doorway peering out, his face pale and drawn and his eyes huge.

'I'm so angry, Billy, I'm upset. Don't worry,' she told him, not stopping but entering her and Restel's bedroom, closing the door quietly behind her and leaning against it, her hands drawn up to cover her burning face.

Billy bought a second-hand push-bike from a shop in Otahuhu. It wasn't too dear and he wanted to ask Seddon to do it up but couldn't because of the tension between them.

Billy would pedal round the local streets in the evenings and at weekends when Restel was not there to stop him going out. It was some time later while he was attempting to put the loose chain back on the bike and making a real mess of it and himself that he met Rewi. Or at least a Maori boy about the same age as Billy pulled up on his bike and stared at him. Billy at first took no notice.

'You got no idea, eh,' Rewi said as he watched. Billy

looked up. He was startled at Rewi's face. Something in his gaze made Billy's mouth go dry. He'd seen the Maori boy about, also riding his bike. They'd stared at each other quite a lot each time. Yet Billy was a loner. Since Jack had gone he was too shook to get friendly with anyone else. There were teenagers all over Otahuhu but normally Billy tried to avoid them. He scowled whenever anyone offered a friendly greeting.

Rewi jumped off his bike and kneeled down on the grass verge.

'I'll do it for you,' he said, grinning, revealing perfectly white teeth. His grin was strong enough to form a sudden glow of warmth in Billy's face.

'Thanks,' Billy said. 'I reckon I'm a bit of a dunce with mechanical things.'

Rewi kept looking up at Billy while he fixed the chain. He even took out one of the links to make the chain tighter, using tools kept in a small leather case hanging from the back of his bike seat.

'This is a bit of a bomb, eh,' Rewi said and laughed. 'It could do with a good going over.'

They swapped names and more glances and soon the sun came out to warm the cold air. The looks passing between them became longer.

A few days after the prayer meeting in the house Restel, having already laid the roughest concrete drive Cushla had ever clapped eyes on, took delivery of several dozen breeze blocks which he used to build a wall along the open front porch. He mixed the cement himself and did the building himself as Colin was now working overtime. The job took most of one Saturday. One morning about a week later when Cushla went out to collect the milk, she tripped on the steps coming back in and grabbed hold of the wall. She'd hardly put any weight on it when the wall simply

161

collapsed. Cushla fell with it, the milk bottles flying up in the air and missing her by inches when they came down. She landed in a heap on the newly sown grass, her nightie pulled up to her waist and her crying out made a bloke across the road laugh out loud before he rushed over to help. She wasn't hurt but was so embarrassed. So riled at Restel later when he hadn't even asked if she was all right. She pushed at him where he stood at the sink in the kitchen. She banged all the cupboard doors until he stomped off to his darkroom, slamming the back door behind him. They weren't speaking to each other at all then, just glaring.

Restel was in his and Cushla's bedroom, sitting on the bed looking through some gospel tracts he was about to place on Billy's bed. He glanced up and saw Billy and a Maori boy biking along the road towards the house. Billy, not noticing Restel watching, got off his bike at the turn-around and let the Maori boy examine the wheel-spokes of his bike. As they both leaned down the Maori boy put his hand on Billy's back and rubbed it. Billy started to laugh. He looked up, his face pink, glanced towards the house and saw Restel watching. Billy went bright red, saying something to his friend. They rode off very quickly. Restel continued to stare out the window. His sight turned inward as his thoughts moved back to that other window in Onehunga and what he had viewed from it. Billy and that strange young bloke, kissing each other in the car. His hands, still clasping the tracts, crushed them.

Cushla received a letter in the early post, offering her a job she'd secretly gone to an interview for at a solicitor's office in Otahuhu. They were so impressed they were offering her more money than they'd first said. Cushla was thrilled to bits. With the others at work the silence in the house got on her nerves, so she went for a walk, had a good natter to some of the women neighbours, then went to one of their homes for a pot of tea and a yarn and home-made sponge cake.

'Good on you, Cushla!' she was told when she skited about the job offer. 'Think what you can shout yourself!' Cushla found out that quite a few of the women had jobs, some part time. It was quite respectable now for women to work. When Restel came home the boost of confidence the job offer had given her and the telephone call she'd made from the public box up the corner, to accept, gave her no worries telling him.

He hit the roof over her news.

'I will not have it!' he told her. 'I've told you before how I feel about women working. You'll write back and tell them you can't. Your place is here in my home, do I make that clear?'

'You can't stop me!' Cushla almost shouted. 'We need the extra, according to you, because of your meanness. I've already told them yes and I'm starting on Monday.'

Restel acted flabbergasted by her determination. He blustered and bossed over her impudence. He quoted scripture. Cushla refused to listen. He was still going at it when Seddon, then Billy, came home. Restel backed off then, went out to his darkroom. Cushla reckoned privately that, for some reason, Restel was certainly a bit scared of Seddon who towered over Restel now, a real man, as tall as her brother, Radley. Seddon had butted in and really stuck up for her, told his dad where to get off, while Billy stood silently in the doorway to the hall.

Restel began to go out more in the evenings after that, after Cushla began her job. She came home full of it and tried to share her days with him but he told her that he wasn't interested.

He had become heavily involved with a group calling themselves the Open Air Revivalists. With them he went

163

round the streets preaching on Friday nights when the shops were open late. Singing hymns and handing out tracts. Seddon and Colin both told Cushla they'd seen him outside the picture house in Otahuhu with several others. They had piano accordions and a banner and spouted the gospel. The banner read, 'Come to Christ for salvation, do not deny grace.'

'I reckon it's a sort of army,' Seddon joked. 'He'll be asking you to make him a uniform, Mum, teaching you to play the tambourine. Glory be! And who the flaming heck is Grace?'

Billy as usual was in his room, where he sat writing poems in the evenings when he wasn't off with Rewi. Cushla was privately pleased Billy had made a friend. She had met them up the road one Sunday when she'd gone for a walk to get away from Restel. Billy was acting a little better lately, though he was too quiet. He'd acted so nervy when she'd said hello to his friend. Seddon had cheered up, though he and Billy still avoided each other inside the house. Cushla reckoned Seddon was taking out a girl, which made her pretty relieved. She'd found lipstick on one of his shirts.

After Cushla had been working at the office for a while and loving it, she went ahead with her newborn confidence and bought a cheap but decent radiogram and a brand new television set on time payment, getting them delivered on Saturday when Restel had taken Colin off to a rugby match out at Papakura. Seddon and Billy made her laugh fit to bust trying to find a good place for the television aerial, even hanging out the window with it. For that one afternoon they let past days slip back in and she reckoned it shook the three of them. She was scared stiff over what Restel might do. It shook her to the core when his reaction was simply not to speak, in a heck of a sulk, ignoring her as he'd ignored Billy for months. Yet that silence began to get on her nerves, kept her awake at night. She covered the television and the radiogram with sheets, watched and listened only when Restel was out, feeling so guilty. After about a week of his silence she became deeply angry that he'd said nothing, felt like shaking him and shouting. She put the sheets back into the airing cupboard. It was an act of defiance.

Billy and Rewi began to spend more and more time together. A closeness rapidly developed, pushing through the aloneness they'd each known before. Billy had more confidence, having known Jack. There was a certain innocence to their friendship, yet it was shadowed by a touch of fear. They felt quite alone and by some instinct did not speak about each other to anyone when they were apart. Rewi had refused to go to Billy's house after that one time when they saw Restel watching. Billy told Rewi only a little about his dad but it was enough. Rewi had seen Restel's face. Rewi couldn't invite Billy to his home because he lived with his gran who had no time for Pakehas. So they would wait for each other beneath a bridge along the Great South Road.

One afternoon, sitting on rocks beside the stream which ran under the bridge, their meeting place, they had touched and kissed each other deeply on the lips and so discovered that what had been going on between them was real, however scary. It was nothing like what had gone on with Jack. And for Rewi there had not been a friend like Billy before, this odd Pakeha boy with the blue eyes who was so gentle and made his heart thud like a crazy wahine's. Rewi was scared stiff that what he and Billy did when they were alone was tapu, was forbidden. Yet their hearts and their bodies sang as they touched and kissed, and the mokemoke, the loneliness of Rewi's living with bad-tempered Gran, Billy with his dingdong family and Rewi with no family at all, his mum and dad killed in a car crash down at Whaka, that mokemoke just flew off like some huge bird. Rewi was koa, was as happy as he'd never felt before. He had a special friend. Someone to watch over and to stick up for. Scared too, just like Billy was. Yet as that time went past and their hearts filled up with this scary joy, their need to share thoughts and hopes and crook things too and simply to be with each other, gave them a delicate courage.

Because Rewi was too nervy to come to the house, Billy used rides on his bike as an excuse to meet him. Restel tried to question every place Billy went to, without fail, mercilessly, in a cold voice which made Billy crook with anxiety. He was forced to lie, for now he reckoned there was something precious he could lose.

Billy still had bike rides round the streets on his own some days when Rewi was busy or had to stay home with his gran.

Billy saw Seddon one Saturday morning in his car and, on an impulse, followed it. Keeping his distance, not taking his eyes off the Austin, Billy saw Seddon park the car down a side road and go inside a tin-roofed, run-down bach from which he didn't emerge. Billy, plucking up courage, and curious, walked up over the grass to where the bach door had been left open, peering in at the gloomy hall. Hearing Seddon's voice Billy stepped inside. He didn't call out. He was too uncertain now in his heart to reckon this was a good idea.

And what he saw there, Seddon lying on the floor with a woman, their clothes scattered about them, kissing and hugging and crying out, affected Billy strongly, caused his aloneness to come rushing back. He fled from the house just after the woman opened her eyes and saw him there, leaping onto his bike and pedalling frantically to the bridge to sit beneath it until the day had almost gone.

The woman came after him in Otahuhu a few days later. Called out his name, took him to a coffee lounge. She talked, trying to explain, telling him who she was. Billy had left after a few minutes, confused and distraught from the way she'd stared into his eyes as if she knew everything about him. He found Rewi two hours later and told him all about him and Seddon with such need for reassurance directed towards his new friend that Rewi cried as Billy cried and Rewi reckoned why didn't they clear out, run off down to Wellington away from all this.

'My gran, Billy, she hits me with a big stick,' Rewi kept saying, trying to make Billy get his mind onto something else. 'She clips me on the ears all the time! She says I'm a queer.'

In the silence which followed Rewi suddenly whispered, 'I think I love you, Billy tama.'

They stared at each other without being able to touch, trembling there at their private meeting place beneath the bridge, faces in shadow with the stream gurgling past. With that word 'love' out in the open it didn't seem too strange, for either of them, after a few minutes. For Billy it all seemed to fit in. His feelings of being different became so clear. And because he was so young he had hope, but without any idea how he'd be able to walk the road along which people like him might have to travel.

Rewi and Billy touched noses, the way Maoris did. They held each other tight and told one another that everything would be all right. Billy told Rewi he would write a poem just for him. Rewi laughed and said he'd make certain Billy's bomb of a bike wouldn't ever get too clapped out. Billy reckoned he'd learn Maori too and write more poems, just for his friend's eyes and his heart.

'Arohanui,' Rewi said. 'Arohanui, Billy. Much love.'

They kissed.

167

It was as dark as pitch when they left the bridge. Rewi said he'd bike home with Billy just to the house, he didn't want to leave him yet and go home to bad-tempered Gran. Billy agreed, for he reckoned Restel might be out.

On the way back from the weekly prayer meeting at church that night the Chrysler broke down and Restel was forced to leave it at a garage and walk home. It was a cold, brilliantly clear night with a sky full of stars and the streets were drenched in moonlight. When he finally reached the house Restel paused, staring at it in a kind of despair when he thought of Cushla, inside. She had almost completely stopped going with him to church now. He was losing each of them to backsliding and sin and filth. Just as he went to close the garage door he paused again, listening. He thought he heard a sound, the moonlight enough to create shadows into which he peered. There came the sound of a sneeze, a muffled giggle, from behind the garage. Restel stepped onto the grass, walking down the side of the garage with stealth, seeing no one until he peered round its corner.

Billy and the Maori boy were standing leaning against the garage wall. Their faces were turned away, their arms so pale and so dark in the dull silver light, entwined. Both had removed their jerseys and unbuttoned their shirts, the jerseys lying on the grass at their feet. The Maori boy had his hands thrust down the back of Billy's jeans. They were kissing. Small sounds came also from their lips, whispered words. Restel stood there rigidly. The boys hadn't seen him. They hadn't heard him. Billy drew up a hand and traced a finger across the Maori boy's lips. The boy took Billy's finger into his mouth, biting it. Billy laughed gently. Restel watched them as his revulsion grew and spread into anger.

*

Cushla was tucked up in bed reading the latest *Woman's Weekly*. She began buying magazines at lunchtime when she walked about the Otahuhu shops. She'd bought a real good book for Billy, a big book of New Zealand poetry. She'd planned to let him have it tonight and was listening for him, hoping he'd get home before Restel. She wanted to cheer Billy up a bit more, now he was acting a bit perky. Perhaps, she thought, one day he'd have his own poems in a book. Cushla ducked her head and grinned to herself, reckoned that'd be a pretty special thing.

Restel suddenly made a choking sound and stepped forward. The boys drew apart so quickly that Billy banged his head on the garage wall. Before he'd opened his eyes Restel had hold of Rewi and was shoving and pushing him towards the road, Rewi's arm twisted behind him. Billy rushed there just as he saw his dad lash out with his fist at Rewi and Billy leaped forward and shoved Restel sideways away from Rewi. Restel turned on Billy then, let go of Rewi, who ran. Restel grabbed hold of Billy by the wrist, unbalancing him so that he fell, dragging Billy on his back across the rough, cracked concrete drive, his shirt rucked up round his neck. Billy started to scream as the concrete gouged his skin through the thin shirt. Restel pulled and jerked his body across the concrete and up the steps into the house. Billy's voice was so loud, filled with shock and pain that Cushla came running from the bedroom, her hands reaching out, Restel knocking her aside with his shoulder. His face had become so distorted Cushla gasped and drew back watching as the two of them struggled and fought and shouted up the hall to Billy's room. Restel almost threw Billy through the doorway before rushing off to fetch the strap. Entering Billy's room without once looking at Cushla and in the darkness in there Restel attacked Billy on the floor. Lashing out at him with the buckle of the belt, dragging him screaming across the room and pummelling his head and face, yelling words at Billy which caused Cushla for one moment to go cold with dread.

Cushla ran into the room shouting, 'Get away from him, get away from him!'

She tried to pull Restel off. Restel twisted round, pushed her out the door so roughly she fell onto the carpet. He returned to Billy where he lay curled up, his arms covering his head. Restel grabbed Billy by his hair, jerking up his head and continued to whip at him with the belt, kicking at his body and legs with the heel of his shoe, the fist holding the belt now pounding the side of Billy's head. Billy with one terrified movement tried to push Restel away, managed to get to his feet in an attempt to escape, got halfway across the room on his hands and knees to where Cushla was struggling to her feet before Restel again grabbed hold. He wrenched Billy by the neck back into the room with such force that Billy was lifted off his feet and thrown against the wall. Billy slid to the floor, the breath completely knocked out of him. Restel, glaring at Cushla, slammed the door shut in her face. She grabbed hold of the handle and shoved at it with as much strength as she could muster. Restel appeared to have locked it. Cushla began shrieking in terror.

From Billy's room there now came a dreadful silence.

Billy lay without movement and without any sound coming from him, in the far corner, lying on his stomach now with his head beneath the bed, having tried to crawl under it while Restel's back was turned. He had passed out.

The following days were perhaps the worst Cushla had ever known. Restel cruelly blocked her from getting a doctor to look Billy over. He threatened her with more violence if she did. He had hauled Billy up onto his bed after the beating, before rushing from him out of the room almost wrenching the door off its hinges as he'd unlocked it and gone into the bathroom. Cushla stood there watching, unable to move as Restel leaned over the sink in there, clutched the sink and vomited into it violently.

Cushla took care of Billy herself, shocked when Billy begged her, weeping, not to get a doctor, he was all right, lying on his bed with the blinds pulled down, his face turned away from her.

Restel had lost control. The following day he took all Billy's poetry and his notebooks and burned them in the incinerator out the back, rummaging through Billy's dresser and tallboy while Billy lay on the bed, facing the wall.

Billy had numerous nasty cuts across the skin of his face, a blackened eye, badly bruised ribs and his back was scratched raw from where he'd been dragged across the drive. Cushla was too sick with worry to feel anger then. She rang up Doctor Hawkins and asked him to come over, while Restel was out at work, told the doctor Billy had been beaten up by a local gang of toughs, which she hoped he believed. Cushla was terrified that he'd ask Billy questions. The doctor dressed the wounds and said nothing was broken. He'd try to look in again but couldn't promise. There was a local outbreak of chicken pox and he was rushed off his feet. In the end he didn't return. Cushla was half-relieved and half-furious at him for not bother-ing. Spending as much time with Billy as she could, she took time off work, as Billy also stayed home. Both him and Restel refused to talk to her about what had happened. Cushla felt almost torn in two by her not telephoning the doctor again to demand attention and not telling him the truth because she was still too scared of Restel's anger.

*

Rewi appeared outside the house very early two mornings after. He stayed there for a long time, staring in, until Restel barged out, spoke to Rewi in a low voice, shaking his fist in the boy's face, and whatever he said terrified Rewi as Cushla watched. He fled. Didn't come back again. Cushla couldn't bring herself to tell Billy. He acted so crook for days and when he did get up it was with a heavy, awful hang-dog look which worried Cushla all the more. She was astounded how quickly he seemed to recover physically, but he hardly spoke and ignored all of them and refused to eat some nights even when she took meals to his room.

Cushla tried her darnedest to get through to Seddon, begged him to have it out with his dad but he shied away, with agony on his face. He didn't even ask what had gone on. She really lost her temper with him and he barged out of the house before she stopped shouting, roaring off in his car and not coming home until the following night and then not until Cushla was in bed, lying in the dark listening for Billy in case he needed her. Seddon's cowardliness made her so wild. She also worried herself sick over Colin. He'd cleared out for a few days then, not telling her where he'd be. It wasn't like her boys at all. They didn't want to know, either of them. She'd no idea what to do, kept planning to go and see the doctor herself, then changing her mind, too sickened at the thought that he might just have reported the incident to the coppers. Fretted that the neighbours had seen. For two nights she slept on the settee in the living-room, too terrified of Restel. She had never seen him like that before. White with hatred, he could have killed Billy.

Every night from then on after he'd eaten, Restel shut Billy in his room, locking the door until he himself went to bed. He pocketed the key until very late at night when he'd unlock the door and leave the key in the lock. Quietly and calmly one night Cushla asked him the details of what haJ happened, insisted that she be told. Restel just as calmly told her to mind her own business. His words brought out the anger Cushla needed. She began to sit on a chair outside Billy's room, before Restel had a chance to lock it. When he tried to get to the door she stood up and shouted at him, tried to shove him away. From that anger which had now come to her, giving strength, he backed off, left Billy alone. Cushla thought she knew what might have happened but wouldn't, could not at that time face it. Restel had yelled the word 'queer' at Billy. She knew what that meant.

'You will not touch him ever again, do you hear me? This is enough!' she shouted at Restel. 'This is killing me!'

Cushla continued to sit there when she could, as Billy refused to leave his room while Restel was in the house. She would try to talk to Billy through the doorway. Billy lay on his bed. Some days now he refused to leave his bed at all and wouldn't touch any food or the cups of tea she made. Cushla would slip out after Restel had gone off to work each morning and ring up both her and Billy's employers, trying to hold on to their jobs. Rewi stayed away and Cushla had no idea where he lived. She didn't see him up the road when she was shopping. She kept looking out for him.

Cushla would sing to Billy softly during the evenings when Restel was out.

'How sweet the name of Jesus sounds
in a believer's ear,
It sooths his sorrows, heals his wounds,
and drives away his fear.'

Cushla clutched at the belief that such words of love

would ease Billy's pain, even as those days and nights moved forward to an event in their lives which was to tear them apart.

Blood of the Lamb

Cushla, weeping, sat at the kitchen table attempting to scrub kumaras, a bowl of water before her. She wept with a helpless despairing gesturing of her hands. The tears flew from her eyes and fell into the bowl. Through the windows streamed ribbons of sunlight which lay across her arms and face as if to comfort her. The early morning frost had gone from the ground outside. The sky was a clear pale blue without a cloud to be seen.

Billy, once her shining light, saved by medical marvel and so special in her heart, had tried to kill himself by slashing open both his wrists with a razor blade from the bathroom cabinet.

Seddon had rushed Billy to Middlemore Hospital in the Chrysler, Billy's wrists bandaged tightly. Cushla had heard Seddon swearing and cursing as he cranked the cold car. The cranking and the swearing had continued for several minutes.

Restel was at a local rugby match, had left early in the morning on foot, not taking the Chrysler. Colin had also gone with some mates from work, refusing to go with his dad. Seddon had spent the morning tinkering with his own car out the front and pieces of it and tools even now lay scattered across the drive. While Cushla was washing windows out the back, leaving the house empty, Billy had emerged from his room and shut himself in the bathroom, not noticing or not caring that the window was half-open. Cushla normally sang hymns while she washed the windows but she hadn't slept well and had felt crook with tiredness since Restel had attacked Billy. Billy was still

175

acting so withdrawn. Restel refused to speak to her at all. When she put the stool below the bathroom window outside, climbed onto it and began to sponge the window down, she didn't immediately look inside.

Seddon heard her shrieking from where he lay beneath the car. He pulled himself from under it and ran up the steps, through the open front door and along the hall. Shouting out to her, kicking the bathroom door open as her shrieking seemed to come from inside. The shock of seeing Billy stark naked crouched over the bath, blood streaming from his wrists, was greater than Seddon thought possible. Cushla was nowhere to be seen. Seddon belted Billy round the ears before dragging him out into the hall, grabbing a sheet from the airing cupboard. Ripping it in half, he tied the pieces round each wrist as tightly as he could. Billy's blood had spurted and splashed everywhere in the struggle. Across the bath, the floor, across the new wallpaper in the hall. Cushla rushing in through the back door reached out to Billy, pulled him to her bosom as he tried to get away from Seddon into the living-room. He'd managed to wrench the makeshift bandages half-off his wrists and as he jerked away from Cushla he fell to the floor onto his stomach, thrusting his arms beneath him. Seddon battled to get hold, to prevent any more blood loss. Cushla was crying out in terror and Seddon was yelling at Billy to be still.

'You stupid bastard, you stupid bastard!' Seddon shouted as he pulled the bandages so tight Billy screeched in pain.

Cushla wrapped Billy in a blanket after dressing him in jeans and T-shirt before allowing Seddon to haul him out to the Chrysler, Seddon shouting at her to hurry. There was no thought that Cushla should go with them. It happened so quickly and then the car not starting and finally it roared off down the road, the tyres squealing as it rounded the corner.

*

176

Unable to enter the bathroom after her glimpse in there, without any idea what time of the day it now was, Cushla had begun to prepare the vegies for tea, banging cupboards and pots and storming about the kitchen as if her life depended on it.

Cushla sat at the kitchen table weeping helplessly, the blood darkening across her bosom and the bowl of water in front of her with the kumaras in it.

Seddon drove the car recklessly. He went through two red lights but didn't stop. Billy was rocking backward and forward, keening in a frightened voice, holding his arms up close to his chest, the bandages remaining in place. As they pulled up outside the emergency entrance to the hospital he fell silent. Seddon half-pulled, half-carried his brother inside. Both of them so pale. Billy was rushed off into a side room. Seddon sat on a chair and began to beat at his head with his fist. His movements were so brutal a nurse ran to him. She knelt down on the floor in front of him and held his arms tightly until he ceased all movement. His eyes stared down at the floor so intently, as if he was peering into the past. Wanting Beth, needing her to be with him except that his shame and fear were too great.

He could not remove what had already happened in the past, and he reckoned Billy had done this to himself because of it. He might not be able to stop what might happen in the future. Seddon felt more responsible for what had happened than any of them and it was as if he could see, just for one brief moment, into a darkness which he had sensed moving towards them for weeks. From the darkness there now rushed thoughts that made his body grow cold. He jerked up his head as his vision cleared, peering over the nurse's shoulder, trying to see where Billy had gone.

Billy watched as the doctor stitched the skin of his wrists together. He felt little pain and wondered why. He had a tube in his right arm and a strange, metallic taste in his mouth. His mind was hazy, filled with cloud and the sound of singing voices. With a shudder that rippled across his skin Billy closed his eyes and let the Maori nurse whose eyes reminded him of Rewi's hold his head to her breast, where he lay on the table.

'Kia kaha, kia toa, iti tahi,' she was whispering. 'Be brave, be strong, little one.'

Billy refused to answer any of the questions the doctor asked. He didn't speak at all.

Two hours later, wrists bandaged, quiet from injections and a transfusion and whispered words from the nurse, Billy sat out in the waiting room. Seddon was told by the doctor that he could take Billy home. The police had been informed. Billy had, under the law, committed a crime. The doctor told Seddon cheerfully that Billy would be better off at home in his own bed, with his family. The local doctor would see to him. No one made any further attempt to find out why Billy had tried to kill himself. Seddon supposed that was up to the coppers, which made him tremble.

'Why the bugger did he do it, mate?' the porter asked, helping Seddon take Billy out to the car.

'Hanged if I know,' Seddon replied, lying. Unlike Billy, who now seemed in control, Seddon was white and still shaking. His eyes stared everywhere except at Billy, now they were together. The porter watched them drive off, shaking his head.

'Bloke that shook shouldn't be bloody driving,' he muttered, turning away.

Billy sat very still, holding his arms close to his chest, hunched over, not lifting his sight beyond the height of the car dashboard. Halfway home Seddon pulled the car over to the side of the road. On both sides were empty sections and remaining patches of manuka bush where houses were due to be built. There was no one about. Seddon leaned across and pulled Billy to him, holding him with a rough kind of love, rubbing his face against Billy's hair, pulling Billy's face towards his and staring at him in a pain which made his head feel as if it was about to split.

Neither of them said anything until Billy whispered so faintly that Seddon almost didn't hear, 'It isn't your fault.'

They leaned into each other, their breathing moist, steaming up the windows of the car. They sat there together for a long time without moving. Outside the car shadows were lengthening, the particular New Zealand light stark. It was still several hours before the twilight would move down to claim it.

Cushla was frantic when they finally got back to the house. Having not even changed out of her blood-spattered frock, she was picking her way up and down the cracked concrete drive, between carburettors and abandoned spanners and spilled oil. She rushed towards the car when she saw it with her hands across her mouth.

A police van was parked on the grass verge.

Like Seddon's, her eyes seemed not able to settle on Billy as he slowly stepped from the car. Billy stood staring at the house. On his face there was a stark stare of distrust.

'The coppers are here,' Cushla told Seddon. Taking hold of Billy's arm, she began to pull him towards the steps leading up to the open front door. Billy was in some sort of trance and passively let himself be taken inside. The two coppers followed, swapping glances. It was now late afternoon. The day was rapidly fading. Several neighbours were watching, not bothering to pretend they weren't.

'It's a hang of a shame, this,' one of the coppers said loudly. He looked embarrassed. Having taken off his helmet his hair revealed a hard line round it and a bald patch pink with sweat.

'He's breaking my heart!' Cushla cried out. She stood in the middle of the hall and cried out to no one in particular. 'It's killing me, this!'

The second copper who had not bothered to remove his helmet was staring at the floor. Billy had walked into the living-room and was sitting on the settee, staring at the bandages on his wrists. Of them all, he appeared to be the calmest.

Seddon began to answer questions. When he spoke he didn't take his eyes off Billy, as if now it was impossible not to look at him. Cushla had gone off into the kitchen. She appeared to be making a cup of tea. After some urgent whispering, Billy was taken back outside and sat in the back of the police van. Both coppers reckoned that Billy would be safer with them, while they sorted it all out. Billy went willingly, a glazed look having taken over his eyes. One of the coppers sat with him, Seddon getting in the front. Cushla came running out onto the porch wringing her hands, coming to a halt at the steps, her mouth moving in a desperate attempt to call out.

'We're going to find Dad!' Seddon yelled at her. 'You stay there.'

Seddon and the copper driving the van spoke quietly as they started off, then fell silent. Seddon had told the coppers all about Restel beating Billy, but not about why.

180

Seddon kept glancing over his shoulder but Billy kept his head lowered. Billy thought of Rewi. Held on to Rewi's face in his mind. He shut his eyes, kept them shut the whole trip to the rugby fields. Soon he could hear his dad's voice, one of the coppers sounding angry, Colin swearing, his dad going on and on in that low, droning tone he used when he preached.

With his eyes tightly shut in the darkness, there moved what Billy thought to be a cold wind and a small thought that the coppers were here to protect him. That they would make changes. Yet something stopped Billy believing that. As the wind grew stronger and pain now edged up from his wrists, the voices around him loud and angry and without hope, he slipped down inside himself, moving away from all sound and all sense of pain and that cold wind until he felt warmth and comfort, and reached a place where there was only silence.

A week went past before Doctor Hawkins reckoned he'd have to commit Billy into hospital. Billy lay in bed without movement and no speech. He dirtied the bed several times. He did not seem to sleep. His limbs had no strength. Whenever Doctor Hawkins lifted one of Billy's arms and let it go, it would flop back onto the mattress. Billy lay with his eyes open saying nothing, staring at the ceiling. Seddon sat beside the bed during the evenings, in an armchair.

Once when they were alone together Seddon whispered, 'Come on, Billy. I know you can hear me. Let's talk, eh?' And then, 'I love you Billy, I never meant to hurt you.'

There was no response.

Cushla kept the book of poems she'd bought beside Billy's bed, for when he got better. She forced her voice to sound cheery and talked to him as she changed the bedclothes and dusted.

'He'll be as right as rain soon!' she told Seddon. Cushla blocked Restel from going into the room at all and he didn't argue. Restel would sit in the living-room reading his Bible. One night Colin finding him there tore the Bible from his grasp and threw it violently against the wall then spat in Restel's face before charging out of the house and slamming the door so hard the glass in it shattered.

Billy wasn't told where he was to be taken. Doctor Hawkins made the arrangements quietly and efficiently and allowed no argument from Restel or Cushla. Billy was dressed, his hair was combed and flattened down with bay rum until it shined. A suitcase was packed and he was put in the back seat of Seddon's car with a blanket wrapped round him to help ease a jerking motion in his legs. Billy sat with his head leaning against the window. Seddon drove the car. Cushla sat with Billy and held on to him. Doctor Hawkins sat beside Seddon. Restel and Colin followed in the Chrysler.

They drove slowly through the South Auckland farm-land, to a hospital for the mentally ill called Kingseat. It was a long journey, perhaps the longest any of them would ever take except for Billy, whose journey had hardly begun. The heat inside the car from a contraption Seddon had fitted was stifling. Billy sat crouched in the corner of the back seat. His legs had stopped their strange move-ments. His body was still. His eyes were quite blank.

Doctor Hawkins began to explain in a quiet voice that Billy would probably be given shock treatment, electro-convulsive therapy, to bring him out of the extreme depressed state he was in. He might be away for quite a while. As he spoke and explained in simple terms what the treatment meant, he stared at Billy intently, leaning over the back of his seat. There was no sign that Billy heard his words at all. Cushla's hands had moved up to her face. She was staring at the doctor as intently as he stared at

Billy. Seddon's hands, gripping the steering wheel, whitened as the doctor's words sank in.

Cushla began to weep. She continued to weep until they had entered the gates of the hospital, moving along the tarmac drive towards the main building. Patients and visitors were dotted across the grass, sitting beneath macrocarpa trees. A cricket match was being played in the centre of the vast lawn, with much laughter. Thin sunlight was reflected off windows. The sky was very blue.

Cushla and Seddon stood apart, in the cavernous entrance hall. There was no sign of Restel or Colin. Seddon whispered to Cushla that the Chrysler had stopped just outside the gates. After a few minutes Colin appeared, out of breath, red-faced and so distraught Cushla hurried over to him.

'Dad's out in the car,' he told her. 'He wouldn't come in, Mum. He's bawling his eyes out like a baby. Struth, I've never seen him like that!'

Cushla attempted to hug Colin to her but he jerked away, sat down on one of the benches by himself. Doctor Hawkins had disappeared down the hall with another doctor. They were left alone. Billy stood beside an orderly who had hold of Billy's arm and his case. Billy stared at the floor.

Cushla began to sing a hymn. She sang softly, just standing there with her handbag clutched tightly to her bosom. She had only sung three lines and her voice stopped abruptly and she looked about her as if she had forgotten for a moment where she was. There was a strong smell of disinfectant where they waited. From behind a closed door some distance off came the sound of someone yelling out. There was a shout, then silence. When Doctor Hawkins came bustling back the orderly, at his nod, began to lead Billy down the hall. Cushla moved as if to give Billy a hug but then she suddenly turned away. The

doctor took hold of her arm. Billy didn't look up. He and
the orderly walked on past doorways in which old blokes
in pyjamas stood staring, with open, toothless mouths.
One of them, with a sharp, coughing laugh, spat phlegm
at the orderly as he and Billy passed by. The phlegm stuck
to the orderly's jacket for a moment. Then it dripped to
the floor.

'In here, me little mate,' the orderly said, opening a
door. 'Soon be clean and tucked up in the ward. You'll like
it here, it's all right. Tucker's good too. I've a real nice
bath ready.'

Billy did glance up, looked back just before he entered
the room. Seddon was the only one to notice. Cushla was
sitting on the bench beside Colin and he was comforting
her. Seddon faltered, stepped back as he drew up his
hand, about to call out to his brother.

Seddon looked into Billy's eyes but all he could see in
them was a dying of the light which had once shone there,
and darkness, having come all the way down the road,
was taking its place. Billy stepped into the room. The
orderly closed the door behind them.

Guilt that Consumes

'He's not mental,' Cushla began to tell the neighbouring women. 'He's just feeling a bit crook. We all do, from time to time.'

She hadn't spoken to any of them until Billy had been shut away in Kingseat for a long while. By then their stares and questions began to plague her. None of the women seemed grateful for her information. They tried to avoid her after that as she had avoided them. One woman who had always been a bit hoity-toity crossed to the other side of the road whenever she clapped eyes on Cushla.

'It's the Lord's will,' Restel told her. 'Let it be a lesson. You are still a Christian, you just turn the other cheek like I have.'

'What do you mean?' Cushla shouted. She had begun to shout a lot through nerves, the doctor had told her. 'You hypocrite!'

Restel glared at her then left the house. He was off to a Wednesday night prayer meeting. How could he, she thought. Cushla didn't go anymore. She had stopped going to church altogether. She spent the time when Restel was out working down the section, weeding her flower beds. She couldn't be bothered growing vegies now. The flowers cheered her up.

They hadn't yet been to see Billy at the hospital. She asked Restel when they were to go. He didn't answer. Later he accused her of having lied to him for years out of spite. He would not mention Billy's name.

'It's killing me, all this,' she'd answered back. 'I've had enough!'

Like tonight, she was often alone in the house. Seddon was out at Takanini working on some cobber's car. He'd told Cushla he wouldn't be home until very late. She wasn't certain where Colin was but she had an idea. His dad would do his block if he knew. Both the boys had drifted off and were rarely home. She knew that Restel, in his heart, accused her of that. Seddon and Colin had accepted the Lord to be their Saviour and now they were turning their backs on Him. Restel had said something of the kind to Seddon recently and Seddon had shouted back that he was more keen on getting boozed when Sunday came round, and to get stuffed. He was working too hard at Victoria Motors, Cushla reckoned. Putting in all those hours of overtime since Billy had been taken from them. It wasn't right. He'd made no effort to try to visit Billy either. By the time Cushla remembered about Billy's job and rang up, they'd employed someone else, were pretty rude over the telephone to her. Cushla was working part time, relieved that she'd been allowed to, just for a few months. She wanted to be there when Billy came home. She'd been thinking of redecorating his room while he was away.

Restel had not gone to the prayer meeting. In the Chrysler he'd driven out to Kingseat. He parked beneath pohutukawa trees near the entrance, sat there and read his Bible and prayed. Then leaving the car he walked to the gates and rang the night bell. Ten minutes later an orderly came along the path shining a torch and calling out. Restel didn't answer but made certain the orderly could see him,

'I've brought this for my son,' he said, holding out a brown-paper-wrapped parcel.

'Oh yeah, bit late, isn't it?' the orderly said, offering a grin.

'I'd be thankful if you could pass it on. I've not come to see him,' Restel said. 'It's a few things he might need.'

'Okay, mate, she'll be right, what's his name?'

'Billy, Billy Bevan. I've written his name on the parcel. I'm not certain which ward he'll be in.'

186

'House,' said the orderly. 'They're called houses in this bin. Pretty flash, eh. Yeah, well, no worries, he'll get this in the morning. Hooray!' and he abruptly turned, walking back along the path, not once looking back. Restel stared past him. Between the trees he could see lights twinkling. He stood there for a long time. Across his face ran emotions he felt unable to control. Anger and disgust and fear and love. The night above him was very dark.

Cushla took to sitting at the living-room window. She would stare out into the road leaving the holland blinds up and the lights off long after it was dark. She would sit there for hours at a stretch and sing hymns in a soft, comforting voice.

She sang for Billy, to Billy, out there in that place. She felt she was being suffocated, but knew she would see Billy soon. She hated this house, detested it. Built on the cheap like Restel'd done everything else in their married life. This house with its pinched windows and the pokey rooms and the awful concreted drive Restel had laid himself. Weeds were growing up through it. She went out some days to look for Rewi, but didn't find him. Billy was in her thoughts every day. She lived to see him again, taking up the past in her mind, blaming herself for everything.

Doctor Hawkins came to see them officially a few days later. He'd telephoned Restel at work to make certain they would all be at home. The four of them had sat down for tea together that night, something they hadn't done for weeks. Cushla laid a place for Billy and stood looking at it in horror as the vegies boiled dry. By the time Doctor Hawkins arrived an awful tension had grown. They were on tenterhooks all the time now. Cushla had cleared the table and placed a doily in its centre, beneath a vase of dahlias. Colin helped her make a pot of tea once the doctor

187

had sat down in the living-room. She had left the sliding doors open so he could look through and admire the flowers, but he seemed withdrawn and she wondered if he might be crook with a cold. It was that time of the year.

Cushla was scared stiff at the doctor wanting to visit. She knew Doctor Hawkins had something serious to say. Her movements were slow, delaying the moment. She dropped one of the cups and felt like screaming, she felt so tense. Colin gave her a brief hug and she tried to smile as she carried the tea tray into the living-room. Restel, she noticed, had his Bible beside him and looked grim, staring out the window as if he wished he was somewhere else. Cushla made a fuss with the tea, getting Seddon to hand round a plate of Melting Moments she'd baked. It was as if they were a roomful of strangers.

'How is he, Doctor, have you seen him?' Cushla asked. 'How is Billy?' Her heart began to thud when she spoke. She sat down heavily on the stool that Kitty had given her years ago. She'd written to Kitty about Billy but received no answer. She didn't know where Radley was living now.

'I drove out yesterday,' Doctor Hawkins said. 'He's feeling pretty crook at the moment, Mrs Bevan.' The doctor looked at each of them in turn, finally resting his eyes on Cushla. She felt a bit put out that he didn't call her by her first name anymore. He acted a bit stuffy, she thought, very formal and cool. It shook her, that.

'You know about the treatment Billy's being given. When that's completed he'll be transferred to what is termed a house. Until then he'll be in a men's ward at the main building. It's quite pleasant. I'm sorry to have to tell you this but his doctors out there will not allow any of you to visit. Possibly later on, when he's responding, but I'm not certain. Billy's quite a sick lad, he needs special attention and care. After your behaviour recently and in the past,' and he looked at each of them as he said the words, 'he needs a complete break. Once he leaves the hospital he may well be boarded out with another family, but I'm just speculating there, you understand. That will be up to all of you. I'm sorry, but the decisions will not be up to me, and haven't been since he was committed. I am in consultation, of course. I'm in total agreement.'

Cushla got to her feet and began to shout. She stood and shouted and shook, her words directed at Restel who was staring back at her. He had picked up his Bible, was holding it in his lap, clutching it like a shield. Colin rushed over to Cushla, put his arms about her. Her shouting stopped abruptly. Her whole body was shaking. Her face was filled with grief.

'I want to see my boy!' Cushla cried out into the silence. 'This is killing me, doctor. Why shouldn't we see him? You can't do this, you can't!'

'I'm sorry to cause you pain,' Doctor Hawkins said quietly. He looked down at the floor, unable now to meet their gaze.

'I took him a parcel of gospel writings,' Restel suddenly said. 'Did he get them?'

Doctor Hawkins went to answer, then shook his head and kept his eyes lowered.

Cushla stared at the doctor's legs. Restel's words caused her face to flush an even deeper scarlet. He'd not told her about going out there. How hairy the doctor's legs were, she thought. He was wearing his usual white shorts and long, pale blue socks despite the weather. For some reason the sight made her calm.

'When do you reckon we will see him?' Seddon asked.

'I've no idea,' Doctor Hawkins answered abruptly, getting to his feet. He was staring at Seddon in distaste.

'I'll be in touch, Mr Bevan. I'll let you all know as soon as I hear anything.' He began to move towards the door.

'I shall take this further!' Restel suddenly shouted. 'He is my son, given to me by the Lord Jesus Christ. I won't allow this, this impudence!'

The doctor paused, then turned back to stare at Restel. After a moment he spoke very slowly and very clearly. 'Mr Bevan, you have no choice. It's too late.'

It was obvious he wished to say more but he quickly turned his back on them and walked from the room. Cushla saw him out. The doctor touched her briefly on the arm.

'Billy will get well, don't you fret about him,' he told her quietly. 'You just try to work on things at this end,' and he smiled before going down the front steps. But he did not see the expression on Cushla's face once he was gone.

After that night they began to avoid each other, Cushla and Restel, Seddon and Colin. Guilt sifted through the rooms of the house like a suffocating dust.

Colin was at the pictures with Ruihi, whose mum had been born in Samoa. Ruihi had been called Lucy at birth but she'd taken that name and squashed it like a bug, she'd told Colin. Ruihi was the Maori name for Lucy. Her dad, who'd buggered off somewhere else, was Maori. Ruihi was fiercely proud of being half-Maori and reckoned she was all Maori, let people think that. She'd told Colin that she thought her own mum was a real dirty bitch anyway.

Colin thought no one in the family knew he had a native girlfriend except Seddon, because they'd seen each other at the pictures with their dates. And he knew Seddon wouldn't tell as he'd been knocking off a married woman old enough to be his mum.

Colin and Ruihi were sitting in the back stalls at the Deluxe in Otahuhu. Ruihi had wanted to go to the flash picture house at Otara but Colin preferred the Deluxe. They sat together in a tight hug, Colin breathing in Ruihi's particular smell, which made him weak with feelings he'd never had for any other girl. From her hair came a delicious scent of an exotic oil. Her hair seemed to shine in the dark. He pulled her face towards his, kissing her on the nose. Ruihi giggled.

'Colin wants to root his sheila,' she whispered, rubbing her hand across his trousers, feeling for his cock. She giggled again. She giggled and laughed quite a lot, which excited Colin, for her voice was low and her laugh sexy. He in turn was stroking his hand up and down the skin of her thighs beneath her short frock, his fingers reaching upward to touch the warmth and moisture of her. Ruihi slapped his wrist, giggling helplessly.

'Watch the pictures, you horny Pakeha,' she told him.

Ruihi was pregnant. She had told Colin a week ago, and he'd felt scared at first, then proud, and now felt so much love for her he wanted to shout it out right there in the Deluxe for everyone to hear. Ruihi had already told her mum, who couldn't have cared less for she was pretty struck on Colin, didn't have a worry that he was in Maori terms a Pakeha, a white boy. She was just glad that Ruihi was happy, despite the troubles it could bring. Family was a good thing, her people found love easy without all the problems Colin's seemed to have had. New Zealand was a real flash country and full of money and jobs after Samoa and she was hoping Colin would come and live with her and the relatives at Otara. She needed a bloke round the place. Her old stinker of a husband had been a lazy good-for-nothing and she was pleased he'd bloody pissed off up north, despite Ruihi blaming her for that. She reckoned Colin would make a pretty keen dad.

Colin sensed that he was liked, loved Ruihi's relatives as he'd never loved his own. He'd spent as much time with them as he'd been able. He was a bit scared what his dad might say or do. Yet he didn't really give a hoot anymore.

191

He wished to get away from home. What had happened to Billy had done that.

Ruihi had wanted to go visit Billy out at Kingseat and couldn't understand why Colin wasn't allowed.

'He's your bloody brother,' she kept saying. 'Boy, it's stupid. No one'd stop me seeing my brother. Some of you Pakehas really stink, you know.'

She wanted to love Billy and already called him her own brother. She had never spoken to Seddon so he didn't exist, but she remembered Billy who had talked to her. Thought he'd been pretty cute and sexy with his big blue eyes and blond hair and smallness. Colin hadn't told her much about Billy's past. He felt too shamed.

After the pictures were over they sat in a bus shelter eating some spare ribs Colin had bought from a new late-night cookshop. It was freezing cold. Colin didn't care anymore that he might be seen with Ruihi. She was his girl, his sheila. He was grown up now. He loved Ruihi. Ruihi loved him. They had rooted, so it was love. They'd had four roots, mostly in a paddock under the moon and stars. One time they'd done it on the back seat of a cobber's car, with blankets round the windows so no one could have a look. There'd been nowhere else. Ruihi hadn't been a virgin, she told Colin she'd had lots of roots, but that to him didn't matter. They belonged to each other no less because of it. He'd begun to worship her. She was the most beautiful creature he'd ever clapped eyes on.

'I'm going to let them know tonight, when I get back,' Colin told her as the Otara bus appeared.

'Want me to come too?' Ruihi asked.

Colin shook his head. 'Nah, Dad will've come back from his meeting all high and mighty,' he told her. 'I'd better do it on my own, eh.'

Ruihi giggled. 'You'll have to, in bed after,' she said and began to giggle even more as Colin tickled her,

192

knocking her juice-laden spare ribs all over the bus-shelter floor.

As she clambered up onto the bus Colin called to her, 'I love you, Ruihi,' and Ruihi turned her head, wrinkling up her nose.

'Taku aroha ki a koe, pakeha boy,' she called. 'I love you too!'

As Colin watched the bus disappear down the road he realized he couldn't remember having stuttered once since Ruihi had told him she was pregnant.

'Struth,' he said aloud, into the dark.

Seddon was sitting out in his car when Colin got back to the house. He'd walked, feeling so good he whistled the whole way. Seddon was crouched over the steering wheel rolling a smoke when Colin peered through the wind-screen. The look on Seddon's face didn't change when Colin gave him a nod. Seddon carried on rolling the smoke. Colin banged on the car roof and grinned, going back into the house. Seddon must be really brassed off, he thought. Colin reckoned he knew why. It was stupid the way Seddon blamed himself over Billy.

Cushla was in her dressing-gown. Unable to sleep she was sitting at the kitchen table drinking a mug of Milo. She got up to make some more and Colin sat down at the table to wait.

'Where's Dad, in bed?' he asked.

'He's out back in the darkroom. He'll be in in a minute.'

'I want to tell you about something, Mum,' Colin said quietly.

Cushla began to bang the cupboard doors.

'Dad saw you tonight up the road messing about with an island girl,' Cushla said. 'He's real angry, Colin. He wants to know if she's a Christian.'

'Ruihi's Maori, she's not an islander.'

Cushla didn't answer. She carried on making the Milo then brought it over with the biscuit tin.

'Seddon's out in his car,' Colin added. 'Boy, he's acting all cranky!'

They sat in silence, waiting for Restel to come in through the back door. Cushla had gone pale. Her hands shook as she lifted the mug to her lips.

'This is breaking my heart,' she told Colin. 'Do you know that? Breaking my heart!' and she started to weep. Colin wanted to hug her but didn't. She was always bawling these days and although he loved her, cherished her because she was his mum, the bawling really gave him the pip as half the time she didn't mean it. When he failed to reach out to her Cushla stopped and got up to wash the mugs when they'd finished the drinks.

When Restel came in from the darkroom in the garage, Colin was so brassed off himself from the tension he was ready for anything. Restel walked straight through and up the hall without speaking to either of them. Before he came back Cushla put her hand on Colin's arm and said in a loud whisper, 'I knew, son. I saw you with her up the shops a while ago and I bumped into the girl's mum when I was coming out of work. She stopped me in the street, she knew who I was! She said not to say. It's all right, son, with me. I don't mind you taking out a native. I understand. But I don't know what your dad's going to do. I haven't seen him so riled since Billy . . .' and she began to weep again. This time Colin leaned over and put his arms round her. They were like that when Restel came back. He had his Bible open in his hands and his face was livid.

Seddon heard the shouting from the car. When he also heard something crash and Colin's angry voice, he leaped out of the car and ran down the side of the house, peering through the windows, his hands making a cave on the glass.

*

Colin had shoved the table over, after he'd told Restel about Ruihi, about how she was pregnant. The news had shocked Cushla to the core. The girl's mum had said nothing of this. Restel had begun to read out loud from the Bible, stood there shaking with anger, his words growing louder and louder as Colin talked. In frustration Colin had pushed at the table with his hands, managing to up-end it, its edge hitting Restel on the legs and throwing him sideways against the stove. Cushla had a second shock when she'd seen the face staring at her through the window, which had made her shriek so loudly the porch lights went on in the house next door and someone came out to have a look.

Restel yelled at Colin that if he didn't give up seeing that islander girl –

'She's Maori, Maori!' Colin shouted,

– that if Colin didn't stop seeing that native girl now they'd done filth together, he would have to leave the fold, that Restel would not have such disgusting sin being carried out under his roof where Jesus Christ his Lord was in command.

Colin lost control. His face twisted in pain as he yelled, 'Then why don't you try and beat me, you bugger, why don't you beat me senseless like you did Billy? Bastard, bastard!' and he threw himself across the room at his dad and Cushla was only just quick enough to grab Colin's arms to prevent him from belting Restel across the head, Cushla shrieking, 'Leave him, son, leave him please!' and Colin shouting every swear word he could think of at his dad, kicking at the table and spitting across it to where Restel leaned back against the stove. Cushla had never seen Colin like this, never.

'Get out!' Restel shouted in the silence which followed. 'Get out of my house! I won't have this, do you hear me? Get out!'

*

195

Colin packed some things into a suitcase, despite Cushla trying to stop him.

'It's no good, Mum!' he kept shouting above her cries. 'It's no blinking good, I've had enough!'

He hugged her, held her tightly to him before leaving the house. Seddon had disappeared. Cushla reckoned Colin might never come back, but that she would see him again. The love they shared inside their hearts would never leave. Restel had shut himself into his darkroom out the back. Hours after Colin had gone and Restel had come to bed Cushla turned from him, kept her back to him all the long night, watching the crack in the blinds for the first sign of dawn.

The following Sunday Restel told Cushla that she was lost to the devil for her encouragement of the boys' wretched sinning. Cushla looked at him with hatred. She felt she had lost Billy forever because of him, because of his cold, narrow heart. Now Colin had gone too.

When he told her for the second time that he would be praying for her she yelled at him, 'I couldn't care less, do you know that? You are killing me, you are destroying all of us! Hypocrite, hypocrite!'

Separate Pathways

Restel was leaving to drive down to Wellington on his new moped for a holiday. He'd sold the Chrysler the week before, claiming it was clapped out. Paid cash for the moped. Cushla reckoned privately that he'd sold the car so he could get away on his own without having to take her. He had told her two days before that he was going, still on his high horse from all the things he'd accused her of, yet still not letting out a thing of any importance. Neither of them had, blocking it off. She watched him from the living-room window and would have laughed had she not felt so crook. The sight of him putt-putting down the street, the moped's saddle bags full to overflowing and on his head that ludicrous child's crash helmet, was humiliating, not funny at all. Whatever must the neighbours think, she wondered. He planned to be away for several weeks, a leisurely preaching trip with stops along the route at Taupo and Rotorua and Masterton.

For a while after he had gone, Cushla wondered whether he would come back. Having failed with them, Seddon scoffed, he was out to save the rest of the country.

'There's still hope for you,' Restel had told her as he'd walked out the door. 'I'll ask the Lord every night to help you back to the fold.'

Cushla had not answered, still speechless after all the words they had shouted at each other. She'd gone out to look for Rewi. He seemed to have disappeared completely.

*

After Colin left home Restel had started to eat his meals out the back in the darkroom. He'd refused to sit down at the table with her and Seddon, even got his tea ready himself when he'd come back from the office. He wouldn't allow Cushla to touch his food. Cushla's job at the solicitor's in Otahuhu brought in a lot more money than Restel's did, so he didn't give her a penny towards housekeeping bills at that time.

'From now on you can get up the shops and buy your own food,' Cushla told him. 'I can't be bothered. You'll see, you'll see how much it all costs!'

Most nights when he wasn't out the back in the garage he'd gone to bed early to read his books. She would listen to the rustle of lolly wrappings. In the tallboy beside his bed he still kept bags of boiled lollies which he sucked as he read his books from the library, where he went every week, taking out travel books. Seddon had told Cushla he hoped Restel'd bugger off to one of the places he read about, if his teeth didn't rot first.

'Timbuctoo for all I care,' he'd said.

Cushla was so humiliated by Restel's behaviour now and so filled with grief over Billy and Colin she remained silent when Seddon made cracks. She could sense that underneath the joking Seddon had really begun to despise Restel, just as Colin had confessed to hating him by clearing out. The reality of that terrified her. For she was, inside her own heart, blaming Seddon for his part in what had happened to Billy. She felt uncomfortable in his company, repulsed. And she reckoned he was a coward. They were all blaming each other, yet not even talking about what they should do about it. A fear that she might soon be alone with Restel if he did come back, and that Billy now was truly lost, plagued her at night.

Seddon sometimes joined Cushla in the evenings to watch the television, after his dad was gone. She was more pleased when he didn't. He would sit and eat a whole cake of chocolate sometimes and Cushla would stew with anger as she watched him. He was terribly unhappy but Cushla couldn't be bothered talking to him about it when she watched him. It was guilt, making him unhappy, as it had grabbed each of them, causing the silence. Except that it seemed worse for Seddon. He spent more and more time away from the house too. She reckoned he was still seeing that woman he'd got to know. Cushla had never met her but had found out about her. She was married, her husband having left her. She was a good deal older than Seddon, much older. Cushla didn't like the sound of that, reckoned it couldn't possibly last. She supposed the woman might make him happy for a while. Not that he deserved even that. Not now, not with Billy still stuck out in that place.

'Your backsliding was responsible,' Restel had shouted at Cushla when they'd faced each other a few days before he'd cleared out. 'All along since Upper Hutt you've let worldly things influence the boys. You've ignored my guidance, not lived in subjection to me as the Lord willed it.'

'It's not to do with me!' Cushla snapped back at him.

But Restel just carried on as if she hadn't spoken. 'I let you talk me into getting that wireless, you took the boys to places Christian people should not enter, you've encouraged them to sin and you've hidden things from me, things about Billy I should have known. Now you've bought that television and radiogram. I'm the head of this house, Cushla, not you. The Lord's at the prow and I'm the captain. If you'd let that alone then all this would never have happened!'

'Don't talk such tripe!' Cushla said. 'You should hear yourself, you should listen to what you are saying!'

After a few minutes of silence Restel continued. 'I know you're running up bills again in Otahuhu, just like you did before. I found out. I won't have it! I totally disapprove of your working. You only had to ask me for extras. From now on Cushla I demand that you . . .'

'I don't care what you want of me,' Cushla said loudly,

interrupting his flow. Restel's face went scarlet. 'I'm a sinner, you said,' Cushla carried on. 'You held that prayer meeting, here in our home, getting your cronies to pray for me. Do you remember that,, do you, eh? You remember kicking Colin out, almost murdering Billy? Where's the good, where's the Christianity in that? I've had enough of your rot. I want nothing to do with it, do you hear, nothing, nothing!'

She was shouting and had gone so pale Restel went to her, reached out, but she shied away fearing that he was about to strike her.

'Cushla, Cushla, you're sick! This isn't you! Can't you see that? The devil's made you do all these things, he's poisoned your mind, twisted it. You've pulled the boys to him as well!'

'I've worked and slaved and fretted to make our boys a decent home!' Cushla yelled at him. 'I have given them love! What have you given them, eh? Tell me that one! What have you ever given the boys except beatings and what they can't do and who they can't see and getting saved, saved! You've shunted us all over this blessed country because you can't hold down jobs, had this place jerry-built so you'd not have to spend money on a real home. You have let my body grow cold and dry because you do not even know what love is, you are not even a real man! I hate you, oh how I hate you!' and she broke down, wept and shook and pulled away from his reaching hands, then suddenly hit out at him with her fists, her eyes tightly shut as he came after her. Restel thumped the air with his open Bible, willing her to go down on her knees and pray for Billy's deliverance from evil filth, pray for Colin and his having fallen away, for Seddon their firstborn rapidly heading the way the other two had gone because he lacked gumption. Going on and on in his droning voice. He touched her with his hands, quoting scripture from the Bible and calling on the Lord Jesus Christ to force her to see the damnation in her heart.

'Leave me alone, leave me alone!' Cushla shrieked, going for him again with fury, ripping the Bible from his grasp and hitting at his face with it, throwing it down onto the floor.

Cushla ran from the room, along the hall and into the bathroom, sitting on the toilet seat after slamming and locking the door, suddenly still in the quiet which followed, holding her hands tightly across her mouth.

Keening for Billy and Colin and Seddon and love.

Seddon was lying on Beth's bed wearing her pink woollen dressing-gown. He was trying to recover from all the beer they'd drunk the night before. Empty bottles lay across the room. Dozens more were stacked beneath the window. Beth had been saving them up. She was going to cut the bottoms off and cement them into a wall she planned to build along the front of the house. Knock down the old paling fence. She'd seen the idea in a magazine.

Seddon's hangover was a real humdinger. He was sweating like a pig and had chucked up twice. Beth tied ice cubes inside a towel, placed them gently on his forehead, before getting dressed for work at the Breweries. Seddon was taking the day off. He was due for a holiday, he told her.

'Struth, do I feel crook,' he muttered, before she left. Beth had been leaning in the doorway, grinning at him.

'Stay here all day if you like, mate,' she told him. 'You deserve the rest. After last night.'

Something in her voice made him raise his head to look at her. She was smiling gently. Seddon attempted a grin, then moaned. Beth walked over to the bed. Kneeling on its edge she lowered her head slowly. Pulling the dressing-gown open she kissed him on the chest, leaving there a mark of bright red lipstick. Seddon reached out to touch her hair.

Their eyes met and they laughed together but then in

Seddon's laughter there appeared a dreadful panic. The sound stopped abruptly and he whispered, 'I love you, mate.'

After Beth had gone Seddon got up and ran the shower, stood beneath it for a long time. Reckoned he should go back home tonight as Cushla might only fret all the more if he stayed out two nights running. He'd leave a note for Beth and see her again at the weekend. They'd planned a cookout down the back of her section with some of Beth's cobbers, despite the weather, hoping to get a few blokes interested in helping to build the wall.

Last night he had been honest with Beth for the first time about the past and what he reckoned had led Billy to try to kill himself. They had lain together naked on her bed as he'd talked. Even though he hadn't set eyes on Billy since his having been committed to Kingseat, the pain and the guilt were still inside Seddon's heart, growing heavy. It took quite a bit of boozing before it would disappear. Last night it hadn't. Beth now knew all about him and Billy. Said she'd always reckoned there was something he hadn't said, some secret thing. And she still loved him. It made no difference. She'd told Seddon that as he'd stared at her in confusion. He'd never met anyone like her. She knew about the sex he'd had with Billy and it made no difference to her wanting him to be there, always, if he wanted. He reckoned she loved him deeply, which astonished him and deepened his shame.

'You've got to forget it now,' she told him gently.

'I can't!' Seddon had cried out in his drunken state. 'I love Billy like a brother, don't I? All that blinking queer business, that's finished with. I don't frigging understand why it happened!'

Helplessly sobbing, hitting at his head, he tried to be rid of the pain there until Beth grabbed his arms and held him

202

still like she was comforting some wild creature that had need of it.

'The whole bloody thing, it's my fault! I may as well have slashed his wrists open myself!' Seddon cried. As the words tore from his mouth, Beth clung to him, she drew his head down to her breasts, letting his lips find solace there, caressing his back with her fingers. Singing to him until he ceased all sound, and slept.

Seddon reckoned Beth should have kicked him out in the morning, been revolted when she'd thought about what he had confessed to her yet she was still holding him when they awoke. Kissed him on the lips as he opened his eyes, held on just as they both had from the moment each had found the other, with some kind of redeeming love growing out of their mutual loneliness and pain.

Seddon had known Beth for only a short time way back when Billy had found them together at Beth's bach, rooting on the floor. The memory of that came to Seddon like a fist pounding his head as he stood beneath the shower. He'd been so hooked on Beth he hadn't given much thought to what it must have added to Billy's state of mind then. It'd been Beth who'd tried to reach out to Billy, not him, even at that time when she hadn't known the facts.

Billy seeing him starkers and lying across Beth, going at it hammer and tongs and moaning that he loved her more than anyone else in the world and crying from what he was feeling in his head. The release of pain and loneliness and the guilt.

Billy had pelted back out the front door. Unable to follow, Seddon had shook and clung onto Beth so tightly it'd taken her breath away. She must have wondered why the heck he'd been so upset. Yet he hadn't said a word to her about the past then. He'd kept it a secret until last night. How the heck was he to have known how Beth would handle what he and Billy had done all those times together? He hadn't really understood much about her for ages. Beth was over forty and Seddon was only twenty-two. She was giving him love but at that time Seddon half-reckoned she might just have been playing about with him, as he'd played about with Billy.

Standing there beneath the shower, he could not cope with what that sight of him and Beth rooting might have done to Billy, with what had followed. Seddon wept in anger.

Beth hadn't asked any questions. She'd told him what had happened when she'd run into Billy up the road in Otahuhu a few days after that. Reckoned that Billy was the loneliest boy she'd ever clapped eyes on with his face so beautiful yet sad. And she'd wanted to hold him to her as a mother would.

Seddon's skin was wrinkled by the time he climbed out of the shower. He sat naked at Beth's table with a bottle of beer and stared out into the yard through the window, feeling like a real rotten bastard.

When Beth got back from work that evening Seddon was leaning over the stove cooking tea. He looked at her a bit sheepishly and she went to him and kissed him deeply on the lips, running her fingers through this thick, curly hair. Smiling gently, staring at the jagged white scar along his arm he refused to talk about, touching it with her fingers. So many secrets, she thought. His family seemed to have made a life built on secrets.

'I reckon I couldn't leave,' Seddon said, grinning his special grin at her.

'Knew all day you were still here. Stay tonight?'

'Thanks, mate. You're a real pal,' Seddon said, leaving the stove and putting his arms about her. 'I love you, Beth. We're together now, eh.'

Later as they sat at the table after tea, drinking beer, Beth reckoned that he might as well move into the bach with her, fetch the rest of his things from home in the Austin sometime.

'You needn't go back at all, not for a while anyway. There's room enough here,' she added. 'I need you. My husband won't be back.'

Seddon, staring into her eyes, whispered, 'Oh Jesus, I don't deserve this.'

'Will you?'

'Yes,' he said, weeping. 'I want to be with you every bloody moment.'

Outside the windows night had come down. Seddon shuddered there in the gloom of Beth's kitchen, re-membering the dark coming down into Billy's eyes.

Colin had taken a chance and popped in to see Cushla. She was getting tea ready for her and Seddon, hoping that Seddon would be home.

'Where's old Moses?' Colin asked, giving her a grin. Cushla hugged him and asked if he wanted a cup of tea.

'He's gone off to Wellington on the moped,' she told him, putting on the jug to boil water.

'What?' Colin began to laugh. 'On that kid's motor scooter? All that way? Boy, what a dum dum.'

'I'll have some peace now,' Cushla said. 'That's all I ask for, son. Peace, and for you boys to be happy and for Billy to come back. He will, he'll be out of that place soon, just you see!'

Colin had kept in touch, had given her a ring at work sometimes and heard all the news and she'd met Ruihi and him at lunchtime one day going into the Plunket rooms for Ruihi's check-up.

'Stay and have some tea, son,' she suggested. 'There's plenty here. Seddon should be home soon. He'd like to see you.'

'I can't, Mum, I have to get back, eh. I'll have a cuppa, though. Ruihi's feeling a bit crook. Boy, I'll be glad when the baby comes. Ruihi moans all the time!' and he laughed, his face going scarlet.

'I must get cracking and knit bootees!' Cushla said, grinning. At that moment she simply longed to talk to Colin, pour out her troubled heart to him as he stood there looking like such a man, pleased as punch that he was to be a dad. Yet it was too hard. Remembering Seddon with Billy on the farm, seeing them being filthy together, Restel treating her as if she did not deserve to be loved, the way he wouldn't touch her. It was all out in the open now. All of it was. They'd asked so many questions out at the hospital when she and Restel finally faced the doctors there. Cushla had denied knowing the Maori boy. She was horrified when she'd found out that Restel had known the whole time about the farm business. He hadn't let on to her in any way just as Mr Young hadn't said, in his letter. Mr Young had told him. Restel slowly beginning to punish Billy, beating him, holding his knowledge inside him just as she had done, but Restel letting it build up until eventually he had completely lost control. Colin still stood there grinning at her then his expression changed until she realized she was glaring at him as an anger began to boil up from her heart. She shook her head and tried to smile.

'Oh, I'm sorry, son, I'm so worn out tonight.'

Colin didn't tell her why he had come, risking seeing Restel. He didn't have the heart for it, looking into her weary, saddened face. He reckoned the strain would be too much. He didn't have the guts. Him and Ruihi were clearing out up north to live on a Maori marae, where Ruihi had more relatives. Ruihi's mum was driving Colin bonkers and they both wanted to leave, him and Ruihi, to make a new start. They'd have the baby in Whangarei before they shifted out to the *marae* further up the coast. Colin knew he wouldn't see Cushla again, at least not for a long time. He tried his darnedest not to show it but something in Cushla's manner made him feel wretched. He sensed that she was a bit touched from all the bad times, the real odd way she'd stared at him for a few minutes, as if he was someone she hated.

It was dark outside when he left. Cushla sat at the living-room window and waved as he turned the corner even though he didn't look back. She sat there and waited for Seddon to come home, humming a hymn to herself and going over and over the past in her mind without being able to control the thoughts.

She was still sitting there peering into the room when dawn came. She hadn't slept. Seddon had not come home. Yet her face had become serene, by the time light crept through the windows. It had come to her like a vision, in the night, what she now had to do, while Restel was still gone. She would leave, clear out like the rest of them were doing. But she would go somewhere far away to make a home for Billy, a place he could come to once he was well, where she could care for him and hold him to her in love, remove all the pain and the memories of violence. She had no choice. She would do it alone.

When Restel returned from Wellington, several nights later, the house was empty and dark and cold. He knew straight off that Cushla had left him. He knew in his heart that he had lost her. The following week, when Cushla did not return, or contact him, he put the house up for sale, along with the furniture. He moved his few possessions to a motel on the Great South Road. He did not seek out any of the family. He remained there alone for many weeks, going to work as usual, until the house was sold to another family. With part of the money he bought a cheap jalopy and caravan and fled south, travelling the country aimlessly, never staying in one town longer than a couple of weeks. His heart remained dark and troubled. Restel was waiting, and as he waited he prayed to his God for guidance.

Each of them was waiting and watching; perhaps Seddon and Colin too, in far-off places, like children flung into separate countries, which continued to keep them cursed by hope.

And Billy? Billy eventually released from the hospital, but still under its care, was boarded out with a family on the North Shore, into a different life that had different rules and different people. His family were to be informed, by letter. Billy also waited, trying to forget, with hope in his heart, that one day he could just walk away from everything, down that road he reckoned people like him had to walk along, to be free, marching to the music of a different saviour. He thought of Cushla with love, yet he felt she was gone from him. She hadn't written. She hadn't been to see him. He had waited for her to come, day after day, until it hadn't seemed to matter anymore.

Cushla finished decorating the tiny spare box room in the flat she had found and was turning into a home for Billy. She'd bought books and a photograph of the poet James K. Baxter she found in a magazine and had framed. On the shelves in Billy's room sat his *Famous Five* books and in Cushla's muddled memory she placed the box of Meccano there, which she'd also saved and taken from the house, certain that Billy had loved the Meccano, that he had played with it often in front of the old wireless which had blown up all those years ago. She planned to write to the hospital to tell them, to let them know her new address, but she did not write to Billy, nor try to contact him. She wanted everything to be a surprise. She wanted a new start for him, once he was free and returned safely to her. Past days crowded themselves like guests into the tiny flat as she waited there for Billy. Convincing herself that he was coming back soon, with a cheerful grin, she invited her new neighbours in for cups of tea and banana cake.

'He'll be home any day now!' she'd say brightly, as the time went swiftly by. She tried not to fret about Restel, nor Colin, or Seddon. She thought only of Billy, there in her new flat, peering from the window as summer began to bloom. She pretended Billy had been on a long voyage, overseas. She even started to believe that, in her heart.

A few days after Billy was taken from Kingseat and had been introduced to his new home on the North Shore, a letter came in the post for Cushla. The hospital's address was written on the back of the envelope. It looked official. She filled the jug and plugged it in, so excited her hands shook. She laughed at herself, ducking her head, checking Billy's room, fussing over last-minute details while the jug boiled away in the kitchen.

'Saved,' she whispered at the doorway of his room. 'Saved!' Then she went back to make the tea.

Morning brightness had gathered outside the window beside where she sat at the table, waiting for the tea to draw, the letter sitting on her lap beneath her nervy fingers. Unable for the moment to read it, sitting there as a shaft of sunlight pierced the glass to touch her face, Cushla was convinced she knew full well what real beaut news the letter would contain. Fretting a bit that she'd have no one to share the news with straight off.

She began to sing a hymn and as she tore open the envelope, her eyes filling up with joyous tears, that shaft of sunlight, becoming veiled by cloud, slowly faded from the room.

Ma Te Kaha Ka Ora
(By Strength Survive)

Pohutukawa trees were to blossom when Christmas arrived with the scorching heat of summer. The sun would yellow the grass and cold rains were to fall as the seasons changed, and time in its indifference moved on. White frost would lie across the earth on clear winter dawns with the sky showing such a deep blue as to make that season seem a lie.

And what from the human heart is called fate, can sometimes grow a wondrous thing. Perhaps it was not to happen from coincidence, but from the touch of some unseen hand, in this country whose true children had named it *Aotearoa*, this Land of Abiding Light.

Beth heard Billy being introduced on the *Woman's Hour* programme while she'd been in the kitchen preparing tea. They said he was one of the most promising young poets in New Zealand. The interview had been recorded twelve months ago when his first book of poetry had been published. The interviewer announced that Billy Bevan had just been awarded the most important poetry prize in New Zealand. In a welter of astonishment, Beth tore into the living-room and turned up the volume of the radio, then rushed to the open windows. Seddon was standing staring straight in at her, through her, there on the fresh dug earth. He had let the garden spade drop. His eyes didn't register her cry, they were inward-looking as he listened. He'd already heard Billy's name being announced, then Billy talking about his poetry. Down Seddon's face ran tears, and with his head lifted, his sight directed now at the sky above their new house, there crossed over his face such shock and a kind of joy Beth climbed out over the window ledge. Dropping down onto the bare earth she ran to him and held him to her. They remained motionless, Billy's strangely adult voice wafting out to them with the sky such a deep blue and the cicadas making such a racket.

'After all these years,' Beth kept saying. 'After all this time, we've found him, Seddon, we've found him!'

It almost seemed that Billy was with them there in the yard miles away from town, where they were living alone.

They left for Wellington as soon as they could, on the Silver Fern train, arriving there in the early hours of a bitterly cold morning. Rain fell steadily. The sky was grey. It was Beth who'd got hold of Billy's address, Beth

213

who organized the trip, convincing Seddon that they should go, using her quiet strength to help him through the long journey down country, when his fear and his guilt began to resurface. He sat the whole trip his face pale, his eyes staring down at his hands that twisted in his lap. Beth did not relax until Seddon fell asleep, his head on her shoulder.

It took several hours to find the house, in an area of the city unfamiliar to them both, and when they knocked on the door a young Maori answered it. He seemed to know who Seddon was straight away, and frowned. He gave them no chance to speak first.

'Billy's crook,' Rewi told them in a low, cold voice. 'We don't want you here, why have you come? You come to have a good look at us, eh? See what the bastards do to us? Billy's crook! Some blokes, they bashed him up with cricket bats and they pissed on him, they carved the word "shit" on his head. Is this why you've come? You come to scoff, have a laugh? Haere atu! Haere atu!'*

Rewi slammed the door in their faces and Seddon stood there with Beth on the steps, shaking like a leaf, Beth not daring to look at Seddon, feeling his body shudder then growing more and more rigid like stone. They stood for quite a while, staring at the door unable to move away. Suddenly it opened again, but Beth didn't recognize the face which peered out at Seddon. It was an old man, wearing a cravat and dressing-gown. The dressing-gown was covered in flower designs.

'You'd better come in out of the wet. I'll put the jug on,' he said quietly without smiling. 'At least you can have a cup of tea. Rewi's told me who you are.'

Seddon and Beth stepped into the gloomy hall and the man closed the door behind them, gesturing for them to follow him down a passage to a large, steamy kitchen. There were two dogs curled up on the floor in front of a glowing woodstove and a cat sitting on top of a table. The

*Go away! Go away!

214

cat stood and stretched itself as they entered. No sign of Rewi or Billy and the house so quiet they could hear the wind outside and the rain beating against the windows. The man stood with his back to them at the sink and began to add to what Rewi had so bitterly told them at the door. He said his name was Errol. He owned the house. Billy and Rewi lived with him.

Billy had been attacked and savagely beaten a week ago as he was leaving a hotel he and his friend Rewi sometimes visited. When Errol finished talking in a tired voice without once looking into their eyes, they were sitting round the kitchen table. The table was covered by a thick cloth on which were printed Maori symbols. On the wall above the table hung a carved wooden tiki. One of the dogs had come across to sit at Beth's feet, staring up into her face with moist eyes, resting its chin on her knees. Beth fondled its ears.

'Can we see Billy?' Seddon asked after a long silence. His voice was low and shaky. 'I've something to tell him. It's about our mum. We've come a long way.'

Errol was sitting with the cat on his lap. It was purring loudly but watching the dog at Beth's feet with rapt attention. Errol smiled briefly then shrugged. He acted unsurprised at their being there, yet they could both see that he was unwell. His face was pale and the skin beneath his eyes was dark. He was very thin. He wore several rings on his fingers.

'It'll be up to Rewi. Billy's in bed. He might come down, if you choose to wait. Rewi will have told him you're here.'

Silence formed round them there in the steam-filled room. After a minute, as if exhausted by his speech, Errol's head drooped and he appeared to go to sleep, the cat now staring up at him with lazy affection. Beth took Seddon's hand, held it tightly in her lap. One of the dogs began to nudge their joined hands with a cold, wet nose as Rewi came into the room so silently he startled both

215

Seddon and Beth. Rewi stood there staring at them for several minutes, a stare filled with an accusing sadness.

'If you're on your own, Billy'll come down to see you, e ora mai nei ano,*' he said quietly to Seddon. Rewi couldn't hide the bitterness in his voice.

He left the room, taking one of the dogs with him. At that point Errol seemed to wake up. He simply lifted his head and opened his eyes without making a sound. Nodding to Seddon, he struggled to his feet and also left the kitchen abruptly, the dog at Beth's feet following him, Errol carrying the cat in his arms.

The woodstove spat, then hissed and was quiet.

'Do you want me to stay?' Beth asked, whispering. Seddon shook his head but didn't speak. She could feel him trembling.

'I'll go out for a walk,' Beth told him. 'The rain's not too bad now. I'll wait down the road.'

Then she added, whispering again, 'Give Billy my love, Seddon. Tell him the news gently.'

Seddon hugged her before she went out into the hall, peering into her face, and the expression in his eyes gave Beth comfort. Then she shut the front door quietly behind her.

The aged timbers of the house creaked as Seddon sat there alone. He and Beth were both worn out, they'd travelled all night on the train and after finding a hotel had come straight here to the house. They'd not heard a thing from Billy all these years after he'd run off from Auckland and now here Seddon was and in this old house here was Billy and they were about to face one another. Seddon's heart was beating like mad. He stared about him as if he sat in an unreal place, wondering who the old bloke had been, wondering at his distant attitude, not showing any surprise nor asking questions. Somehow that added to the

*Up to now he's still alive.

216

unreality. Seddon froze when he saw a photograph of himself sitting on the ledge above the woodstove. One Restel had taken years before. Seddon's face, though much younger in the photograph, staring out into this room made him uneasy. He could hear no sound from the rest of the house, as if there was no one in any of the other rooms. A battered alarm clock ticked loudly where it stood also on the ledge above the stove. The room was clean but cheaply furnished. Rag rugs lay across the unpolished floor. In the corner, on boards across a lumpy armchair, sat what looked like several wet clay busts, their faces turned away.

Seddon suddenly wanted to clear out, leave like Beth had done. An awful shame began to grip his heart. Yet he clutched the arms of the chair and did not move out of it.

Beth had tracked down and bought one of Billy's slim books of poetry. Seddon realized it would still be with her, inside her handbag. As he continued to sit there he feared that this whole visit might be a stupid mistake and that his intentions now were selfish, after what he'd been told. Raking up the past would be foolish. Now, him and Billy were different people. Too many years had gone and he didn't belong here. He should not have let Beth go off alone like that.

He didn't see Billy appear in the doorway at first, to stand looking at him. Seddon was staring at the floor. Billy wore a blue sports cap pulled down low over his forehead and the skin round his eyes was swollen and bruised. He was tucking his shirt into his jeans and didn't move again until Seddon, startled by the woodstove spitting, raised his head and the two stared at each other.

'Why have you come here?' Billy eventually asked. He stepped fully into the room and sat down at the table opposite. He kept his head lowered slightly as he spoke and Seddon could barely see his eyes.

'We heard you. On the radio. Beth rung up. They gave us your address. So you're a poet?'

'Yeah,' Billy said with a short laugh. 'They say I'm to be famous.' Then after a strange smile he added, 'Errol said you had something to tell me, about Mum?'

Billy's voice was so confident, deeper than Seddon could ever remember hearing it.

Seddon didn't reply straight away. When he did he said simply, 'Mum had a stroke, Billy.'

Billy turned his face away for a long time. Then he asked, 'How bad?'

'She's paralysed down one side. She can't talk very well. She's all right, she's in a nursing home. Beth and I reckoned you might want to come back up with us and see her. Each of us has now. Even the old man. None of us knew where you were, all these years.'

Billy drew up his head, revealing fully his bruised and injured face. Without fuss he pulled off the cap and stared across at Seddon without any expression in his eyes except for a mild curiosity. Seddon drew back sharply in his chair and as he looked his face muscles contorted.

'Oh Christ, Billy, oh Christ. What bastards did that to you?'

Billy looked away from his brother's gaze and shrugged.

'Strangers. They were in a hotel we sometimes go to on the other side of town. They followed me after I left. I'd been out on my own. The hotel is where some of us meet to relax. It's not as bad as it looks. Rewi's looking after me. And Errol. He found me,' and he smiled, as if to himself.

Then he added, 'I'm sorry about Mum but I can't come up to Auckland right now looking like this.'

'Did you go to the cops?' Seddon asked.

Billy laughed and made a throw-away gesture with his hand. His laugh held a bitterness which shook Seddon. For a while they just stared at each other then Seddon asked, 'Why didn't you ever contact Mum?'

Billy didn't answer. He stared down at the table, his face going red. When he did speak it was almost in a whisper.

'Too scared, I thought she hated me. She never came to see me, never wrote. None of you did. All that time in hospital. I just wanted to get away after that. I didn't reckon any of you cared a shit.'

There was another, longer silence before Seddon falteringly began to speak.

'Mum sits all day at a window in the nursing home, eh. She looks out at the road. Whenever she sees anyone passing, she leans forward and peers through the glass and she tries to smile but then the smile stops and she'll sit back and say in a real strange voice, "Not this time, Kitty, not this time, Sister." The matron at the home told me that, Billy. They can't stop her doing it. We went to visit, Beth and me. Mum became so angry she tried to shove her tallboy over and banged its doors. She thought I was Restel and I was asked to go. The matron said she sits and waits for you. She'd been waiting for years in her flat for you to show up but the strain was too much and she had a stroke. You just buggered off from Auckland without a word and look what it's done to her.'

As Seddon said the words, he kept his eyes lowered and his hands in his lap would not be still. They pulled and pushed at each other, strong hands yet now so white it was as if the blood had been drained from them as it had from his face. It was the longest speech he'd ever made to anyone. After he stopped speaking Billy leaped up from his chair. He began to shout. He shouted and swore and cursed for minutes, while Seddon remained not raising his sight, letting the words bash at him. But when he did lift his head his eyes were streaming with tears. Billy's shouting faltered and died. Without either of them hesitating, they stepped towards one another, Seddon's chair falling back with a crash as he got to his feet. They embraced and held on to each other so tightly and with such strength it tore the breath from their lungs.

*

219

They were still standing like that when Rewi and Errol both came back into the kitchen, closely followed by the dogs. Billy drew back then, released the hold he had on Seddon and went to stand beside Rewi, and all four stared at each other as if Seddon had only just stepped into the room. There was a change in the air, a lowering of tension. Billy and Rewi without removing their gaze from Seddon began to speak to each other in Maori, softly, while Errol with a kind of grin moved across to put the jug on for fresh tea. Rewi still looked at Seddon with wariness as they sat down at the table.

'This is Billy's family now, eh,' Rewi said and spread his arms to include the dogs and Errol. He grinned at Seddon for the first time.

'We look after each other. We try to keep out the stink. Sometimes it finds us,' and he reached out and gently touched the wounds on Billy's forehead. Rewi looked at Billy with what Seddon reckoned was a deep love. It was a look which Beth often gave him.

Billy had not pulled away, when Rewi touched him.

'I fix that the Maori way,' Rewi said, turning his gaze to Seddon. 'I love your brother, Pakeha. He is my man and my woman and my mate. Same goes for him, E Billy tama. Ma te kaha ka ora.'* Then he whispered, 'Errol lets us live here. He's one of us. We love him and he loves us.'

There was no need to talk any more about what had happened in those lost years. Billy and Seddon looked at each other and knew that. Except that Seddon told Billy and Rewi how Beth and he too were different. Beth had got treated so rough because Seddon was young enough to be her son, which had made some people sick. They too had gone away to a place where they could live in peace. Billy and Rewi and Errol smiled at his words, yet sadly.

*By strength survive.

'Will you come up to see Mum?' Seddon asked. 'She loves you, Billy, she always has loved you like anything. Beth and me'll put you up.'

He paused, fighting to control his unsteady voice.

'Colin's been down, with Ruihi. They've got a little girl, Billy. They send their love, eh. Dad did too. Dad's changed, you've got to believe how changed the old man is . . .' Seddon stopped speaking, drew up his hands and covered his face. No one moved. Seddon gave out a long shuddering sigh. He began to weep then stopped suddenly. 'We all need to see you,' he whispered. 'We love you too, Billy.'

'If I come I'll come with Rewi and we'll stay with our friends,' Billy said, so softly that Seddon, looking up, had to lean forward to hear.

The dogs had fallen asleep in front of the woodstove when Seddon got up and reckoned he'd better get off and find Beth. She'd be freezing out there, waiting for him.

Billy just said, 'I didn't want her to see me, Seddon,' and Seddon nodded. He shook hands with Errol and then Rewi who for some reason looked away as their hands gripped. Rewi stared across into Billy's eyes. He didn't speak.

Seddon and Billy hugged out in the hall once they were alone. Seddon whispered, 'I'm sorry, oh Jesus, I'm sorry,' as he held Billy to him. They said nothing as Billy opened the front door, for so much had also been spoken through their eyes and in them now there was an absence of pain, there was no anger and no shame but yet a sadness rested there.

It had been bucketing down with rain when Seddon and Beth had arrived at the house. Now as Seddon left it the rain had stopped and thin sunlight drenched the street and the pavement. He had only moved a few yards down the road when something forced Seddon to turn and look back. There was Billy standing in the open doorway, his cap clutched in his hands, and through some trickery of

221

the light which shone down his face was without blemish and the skin across it was smooth and his eyes sparkled. With that vision of his brother in his own eyes, Seddon marched off down the road towards Beth, the person who had saved his own life and whom he also loved and cherished with his heart.